Spirit in Time

by

Julie Howard

Spirited Quest, Book 3

Spirit in Time

Cover Art by *Kim Mendoza*

The Wild Rose Press, Inc.
PO Box 708
Adams Basin, NY 14410-0708
Visit us at www.thewildrosepress.com

Publishing History
First Fantasy Rose Edition, 2021
Trade Paperback ISBN 978-1-5092-3510-0
Digital ISBN 978-1-5092-3511-7

Spirited Quest, Book 3
Published in the United States of America

"Are you a ghost?" A young girl stood where the guard had been only minutes before. She spoke matter-of-factly, her dark eyes alive with curiosity.

The house was still whole, she was alive, and the world hadn't ended. Jillian scanned the room for damage, then blinked. This must be a dream. The long dining table—bare just moments ago—was now laid for a meal. Glasses sat upright, forks and spoons lined up in perfect order, and a tall flower arrangement appeared unscathed. A crystal chandelier above the table remained perfectly still.

The guard and Asian man were nowhere in sight.

The girl, dressed neatly in a calf-length white pinafore embellished with pink ribbons, didn't appear rattled by the cataclysmic jolt.

"What happened?" Jillian asked, still crouched on her knees. "Are you okay?"

"You don't belong here. Mother will be angry."

Even though the floor had ceased to shake, the roiling continued in her head. Might this very real looking girl be a spirit? Most apparitions wavered in some manner, their appearances paler and *less there* than the tangible world around them. This child appeared solid in every way, from the tips of her shiny chestnut hair to the toes of her lace-up black shoes.

Praise for Julie Howard and...

HOUSE OF SEVEN SPIRITS:

"What a great mystery! Ms. Howard combines suspense, romance, vengeance, and ghosts to weave a story that's engrossing from page one."

~InD'Tale Magazine "Crowned Heart" review

SPIRITED QUEST:

"One of those 'make you feel good' kind of books. Julie Howard is an author to check out."

~Long & Short Reviews

WILD CRIME:

"Wild Crime is one of the best mysteries I've read in a long time. Julie Howard is a brilliant mystery writer who leaves clues for the reader, like breadcrumbs. Fans of Mary Higgins Clark and James Patterson will love this suspenseful thriller. Highly recommend!"

~N.N. Light Book Heaven

CRIME AND PARADISE:

"Oh my gosh, one of the best books I have read in a while."

~NetGalley (5 Stars)

Dedication

For those who love to imagine the impossible

Acknowledgments

I'd like to thank the wonderful team at The Wild Rose Press, and especially my amazing editor, Kaycee John, who has now skillfully guided me through several books. I am deeply grateful for her advice on where to cut long-winded passages and when to supplement the action. She always seems to be right – a great trait in an editor.

I'm also grateful to my critique group in Boise, Idaho who always provide unflagging support. Through some pretty wretched months of 2020, our small group of dedicated writers continued to meet – in person at a local park or via Zoom. Thank you Kim, Ben, Laura J., Connie, and Laura W. for helping me hone early drafts of this story, and always putting the writing first.

Chapter One

There had to be a ghost or two in Sacramento.

Jillian Winchester hiked her backpack higher on one shoulder and marched out of the train station. She had bungled her train time—and mistakenly showed up at 7:30 *a.m.,* instead of 7:30 *p.m.* What a ridiculous mistake. Now, stuck in this way-station city and caught between her home in Mendocino and her destination in Nevada, she had little to do for twelve hours.

Except…Sacramento had a remarkable history …and history always meant ghosts.

She might utilize her time with a bit of exploration and dredge up a paranormal post for Spirited Quest, the blog that was also her business. A very nice business too, thanks to thousands of dedicated fans of her supernatural adventures and the advertisers who sought their attention. Her website grew in popularity daily, earning her an enviable living, and driving her on a constant hunt for compelling stories. Such as the silver-boom era madam rumored to haunt Virginia City, Nevada, the destination of her train trip.

As a result of the delay, the madam would have to wait. One advantage to being your own boss was the ability to work how and where you wanted. From the deep pocket of her ankle-length peasant skirt, she withdrew her phone with the intent to call her boyfriend, Mason. Seven a.m. He'd caught an overnight flight to Brazil for an assignment to photograph sea turtles for Extreme Nature magazine. He wouldn't land for another hour or two. Her heart sank. An entire week, seven long days, until he returned.

A hairy arm shot out and blocked her path. Startled, she drew back. A homeless man, with gray whiskers and bleary eyes, stared at her from the train station's shadow.

"Have any spare change?"

"Sure." She dropped the phone into her pocket, then dug a few bills from her wallet. The man must have slept nearby, most likely on the hard concrete. Some people had more difficult problems than a train schedule mix-up.

He tipped an imaginary hat to her. "Thank you much, ma'am."

The old-fashioned courtly gesture drew a smile to her face, and she paused. "Do you know of a café nearby? I have a few hours before my train."

"The Cuckoo Clock is my favorite. Henry saves a day-old muffin for me every Wednesday." He gestured down the street. "Three blocks that way on the right-hand side."

She dipped a curtsy and his chuckle followed her as she headed toward the café. Many believed a plea for spare change was a scam, but did it make sense to help the dead if she ignored the living? A little kindness went a long way.

Cars flew past on a nearby freeway, commuter traffic ebbed and flowed, an early jogger huffed by on the sidewalk. The warm mid-May morning promised a sweltering inland-California afternoon. A lavender lemon tea would be perfect to kill an hour or two while she people-watched and caught up on email.

Then she'd play tourist and see if she might rustle up a spirit or two.

****

After a couple of hours bent over her laptop and two cups of tea, the city beckoned. She paused by a table of older men with the appearance of longtime friends who met for coffee once a week.

"Good morning," she said. "I'm curious about Sacramento's history. Do you have any suggestions for a visitor with a few hours to spare?"

The three men sat up in interest.

"There's the old railroad museum or Sutter's Fort, built when this area was still part of Mexico," one offered.

Another, with a neatly trimmed beard and a professorial appearance, waved his hand. "I like the old Victorian mansions, the painted ladies of downtown."

Both recommendations promised intriguing spots to find ghosts.

The third man, the eldest of the three with thin white hair, cleared his throat. "You can't go wrong with the Crocker Museum. There's a bit of everything inside. A historic mansion, fabulous artwork, and it's close by." He raised a shaky finger. "The past comes alive for me whenever I go. The museum's a local favorite."

A small thrill rippled through her at "the past comes alive." Wasn't this exactly what she sought? "Thank you for all these ideas. I may start with the museum this morning. Where is it?"

They gave directions, assuring Jillian it was but a twenty-minute walk away, then waved goodbye. As she went out the door, their voices followed her as they debated the different options for directions.

She wandered on foot past the old public library and city hall. The spring weather and mature shade trees on every block made for a pleasant stroll. Although she grew up in California, and now lived on its north coast, she'd only been to the state's capitol city a few times in her life. Once, in the fourth grade, a segment on state history prompted a field trip to the grand domed Capitol. Her class had picnicked in a park and ate saltwater taffy in Old Sacramento, a section of town where riverboats once docked on their way to San Francisco. The city, though not as famous as its Bay Area neighbors, boasted a colorful and important history of its own in the formation of the country's thirty-first state. Modernity and the past resided side by side here, parallel times that blurred at the edges as old buildings flaunted updates and hundred-year-old oaks graced modern city parks.

The city had to have noteworthy ghosts, from gold-rush miners to railroad barons. Past the downtown buildings, stately Victorian houses presided, some well-tended and others dilapidated from decades of neglect. In her imagination, horse-drawn carriages rolled down the street, women held skirts out of the mud, and men wore pistols on their hips.

Across the street a shadow flickered, drawing her attention. Before her stood a three-story mansion, backed by two even larger structures, all connected by covered corridors. A sign read: The Crocker Museum. A cloud crossed the sun, momentarily casting the mansion in darkness. At a second story window, a face materialized. A man with distinct Asian features stared directly at her, sending a sharp prickle of electricity up her spine. A rumble sounded underfoot, as if a non-existent subway line existed below, but the noise dissipated just as quickly. The man in the window raised a hand as though beckoning Jillian to join him. She blinked—only once—but he vanished.

Her heart beat a little faster as she headed toward the farthest building, the modern entrance to the museum. A haunted mansion was right up her alley. Old buildings and their former inhabitants created excellent blog posts, and this one might make up for the mistaken train schedule. She paid her fee and left her backpack in a locker as directed. She stuck a visitor badge on her blouse and studied the exhibit map.

Jillian usually avoided museums. Disturbing energy flowed from the various relics accumulated from myriad cultures and eras. Nearly every display that contained antiquities was prone to contain old weaponry, and these exhibits she avoided. Moans and screams emanated from these implements. Brutal deaths never ended; intense suffering changed the atmosphere at an atomic level and lingered forever. Two summers ago, in the Duomo Cathedral in Florence, Italy, she had joined a tour that climbed a narrow inside passage to the top. Normally spirits didn't frighten her, but these ghostly hands grasped at her ankles and tugged at her hair. Nightmares haunted her for weeks afterward.

A young woman with pink hair, a nose ring, and a docent's badge approached as Jillian hesitated. "Can I help you with anything?"

Explaining her quandary about tortured ghosts and antiquities would take too long. Anyway, she was curious about the man at the window. "Is the house part of the museum?"

The woman stood straighter, proud in her knowledge. "Absolutely, and you won't want to miss it. It's the original house owned by E.B. Crocker and is a wonderful example of Italianate Victorian design." The words flowed out as though the docent had waited for someone, anyone, to ask her a question. "E.B. Crocker was one of the most powerful men of the late 1800s Gilded era—California supreme court justice, attorney for the Central Pacific Railroad, and prominent banker. His wife, Margaret, loved to collect art. They built a gallery—the middle building in the complex—to display the work."

"History major?"

The docent giggled. "Pre-med. But I've worked here for two years. I know enough to write a book on the Crocker family."

An older couple lingered nearby, waiting their turn to ask a question, so Jillian rushed on with her main concern. "No, uh, weapons or stuff like that. I'm just here to see the house."

The woman gave her head a vigorous shake. "Vases, paintings, some furniture. No weapons I can recall. Make sure you visit the second building, the grand gallery built by the Crockers, which has a fabulous staircase and ballroom. You can only tour part of the family mansion, like the dining room. There used to be an ice rink, bowling alley, and a billiards room, but those rooms are closed to the public." She pointed to the elevators. "Follow the signs." And nodded to the next visitors who awaited her attention.

Jillian's flat ballet slipper-style shoes pattered over the tiled floor as she angled from one hallway to the next. Whispers trailed after her as she hurried past an old Native American dugout canoe and a display of Japanese ceramics. One had to be determined to get to the house, a fair trek at the farthest point from the museum entrance. The museum flowed directly into the grand gallery building, connected by a long corridor and through a high arched doorway.

The decor transformed from sterile white modern to the dark heavy wood of a bygone era. A light lemon polish scent permeated the air. Three stories high and anchored by double curved staircases, the nineteenth century gallery and ballroom must have seen elegant parties and numerous dignitaries. It would have been a showpiece of wealth and prestige.

Few visitors roamed this part of the museum. Jillian soaked up the atmosphere and enjoyed the tranquility. She strolled along, more interested in the carved woodwork and architecture than the displays. No spirits spoke to her, but that prickling sensation at the back of her neck continued. Someone from a previous time remained in this house.

An older man somewhere north of seventy, with beautiful silver hair and warm brown eyes, stood in a corner of the ballroom. Around his neck hung a guard's badge. "Early bird. There's been a handful today."

She flashed a smile at him. "I flubbed my train schedule and am now glad of it. This is a lovely museum."

"General Grant danced on these floors." He made a grand gesture toward the middle of the room. "If this house could talk."

Her shoes squeaked slightly on the well-polished floor, and for a moment a swell of music echoed before it vanished. Heavy brass chandeliers hung from the gilded coffered ceiling and intricate painting covered the wood. It was easy to imagine the sweep and rustle of taffeta skirts and whisper of slippers, the low murmur of conversation amid cigar smoke, and bright tinkle of crystal glasses.

"I imagine this house has a remarkable history. Any ghosts?"

He gave her a look of disapproval. "Reality is much more interesting than ghost stories. You want to see something noteworthy, go to the central staircase." The guard pointed to the other doorway, across the room. "My favorite painting is there, commissioned by E.B. Crocker in 1872 to warn the public of the wicked nature of the mining camps."

He led the way to the mansion's main curved staircase. The large piece, titled "Sunday Morning in the Mines," caught her eye. She smiled at the vivid and rowdy characterization of a gold-rush camp.

"The right third of the piece illustrates how men can behave themselves properly." The guard pointed to where three men read the Bible. "There, a man in a cabin writes a letter, surely to a loved one back home. You see two others wash their clothes." He swept his hand to the left. "Here we have men engaged in horse racing, drunkenness, and brawls. Consider the significance of the artist dedicating two-thirds of the piece to sin."

The guard stepped back toward the ballroom, enabling Jillian to study the artwork on her own. She enjoyed the intense colors the artist used, the attention to detail, and humor and pathos. The ruddy cheeks of the drunken miner, dirt-crusted knees, and...

This was so strange. She edged closer, craning her neck to study the picture in greater detail. Among the sinners on the left, a familiar figure stood. A small smile crept to her lips and then faded into a frown the more she stared. The likeness to her boyfriend, Mason Chandler, was beyond striking. The same light brown hair and tall strong frame, but more than that, the figure had the same stance, the exact way Mason cocked his head when puzzled. Remarkable.

The painting was too high, making the figure too small for scrutiny. She retrieved her phone from her skirt pocket to snap a picture in order to later share the quirky coincidence with Mason. He'd likely landed in Brazil by now.

The guard's deep voice rose sharply. "Excuse me, miss, no pictures in the museum."

Startled, she spun just after her finger clicked the button and the automatic flash lit up. "Oh, I'm so sorry. I forgot."

Museums always frowned on photography, especially with a flash because repeated exposure to light faded the paint. How compelling that this likeness to Mason made her forget this rule.

The guard glared and didn't budge from his spot until she pocketed her phone. Face warm with embarrassment, she climbed the stairs with just one last glance at the artwork. So strange. Mason—or an ancestor of his—might very well have been the model for the artist.

With a sense of unease, she continued past the ballroom through a long hallway that led to the original house, out of sight of the guard. With each step, a sense of foreboding increased. In a room with a long, bare dining table and display cases along the walls, she stopped to examine the picture on her phone. The likeness was striking, as though Mason lived in another place and time. As far as she knew, no branches of the Chandler family lived in the United States. His family hailed from Australia, and long before that various parts of Europe. Of course, an adventurous ancestor may well have joined the gold stampede to California to seek his fortune.

She tapped on her phone: *Check out the fellow on the left.* She attached the picture to the text and sent it off to Mason. A red exclamation mark popped up, with a note: *Message not sent.* Annoyed, she wandered to a window that overlooked the street below. Sometimes large structures obstructed cell service. Standing beside the glass, she tried to send the text again and received the same response. The guard entered the room, his pace slow and steady. He spied on her without being too obvious, a skill he must have honed over years of guarding the museum's treasures.

"I haven't taken any more pictures," she volunteered in an effort to head off any more warnings. "I wanted to send a text. Is there a problem with cell service in here?"

"Not at all." He parked himself at the other side of the room and observed her without really watching her.

Determined now, she restarted her phone and tried again with the same result. Ridiculous. She dialed the number.

"Hullo?" A man's voice barked into her ear. It was not Mason.

The number displayed on the phone was correct. Grateful she hadn't misdialed, she hesitated for a moment, then said, "Uh, hi. This is Mason's number. Is he there?"

"You have the wrong number."

"I don't think so."

"Lady, I've had this number for two years. I should know my own number by now." The phone clicked as the man hung up on her.

She studied the phone to reassure herself she hadn't made a mistake. "This is odd. There must be a glitch in the system today."

The guard strolled toward her. "Ma'am, please don't lean against the woodwork."

This fellow took his job seriously. She hadn't even touched the wall. She opened her mouth to tell him this, but his image wavered. Another man stood directly behind him, the Asian man she spied in the window earlier, pale as death. The rumble beneath her feet returned. Simultaneously, the world tilted and the floor lurched up. A deafening crack sounded, like the shudder of splitting wood. She tumbled hard to her knees, dropping the phone. Panic surged through her.

An earthquake. A big one.

She scrambled to the doorway past glass display cases as the house rolled one way, then the other. Bile rose in her throat. Instinct screamed at her to run, to get outdoors, but a lifetime in earthquake country stifled the impulse. The worst action you could take in a tremblor was to run pell-mell through a building, especially one laden with heavy chandeliers and glass cabinets. Doorframes were stronger than a ceiling and she needed a safe harbor fast. She grasped the thick wood frame, tucked her head between her knees, and prayed the back-and-forth roiling wouldn't crack the house in two.

Never before had she experienced a quake of this magnitude. The heaves and rolls continued for at least a minute. She'd been through seismic throes many times. Most hardly worth mention, with a small jolt or gentle roll like the wake from a small watercraft lapping against the shore. On occasion, only the mild sway of a suspended lamp indicated a quake in progress. Never had she been knocked off her feet.

Her stomach continued to churn even after all went still. She lifted her head and sat back on the floor to survey the damage to the museum. So many beautiful, rare objects, but no broken glass strewn across the floor, no alarms or sirens in the distance. She figured the massive table vase in the next room must be glued down, display cases secured against the walls, as she hadn't heard a crash. More peculiar, not even the chandeliers swayed.

But wait. Something else was different. No, that wasn't quite right.

Everything was different.

Chapter Two

"Are you a ghost?" A young girl stood where the guard had been only minutes before. She spoke matter-of-factly, her dark eyes alive with curiosity.

The house was still whole, she was alive, and the world hadn't ended. Jillian scanned the room for damage, then blinked. This must be a dream. The long dining table—bare just moments ago—was now laid for a meal. Glasses sat upright, forks and spoons lined up in perfect order, and a tall flower arrangement appeared unscathed. A crystal chandelier above the table remained perfectly still.

The guard and Asian man were nowhere in sight.

The girl, dressed neatly in a calf-length white pinafore embellished with pink ribbons, didn't appear rattled by the cataclysmic jolt.

"What happened?" Jillian asked, still crouched on her knees. "Are you okay?"

"You don't belong here. Mother will be angry."

Even though the floor had ceased to shake, the roiling continued in her head. Might this very real looking girl be a spirit? Most apparitions wavered in some manner, their appearances paler and *less there* than the tangible world around them. This child appeared solid in every way, from the tips of her shiny chestnut hair to the toes of her lace-up black shoes.

She had experienced strong visions in the past, in

which she inhabited a halfway world—a place somewhere between past and present where she met spirits who sought her help. These events occurred without notice, triggered by an item she either touched or smelled. This must be what happened, a flipping of worlds soon to right itself. Her sudden appearance surely frightened this child, as would her impending disappearance.

She struggled to her feet and braced her hands against the wall to steady herself. "I'm not a ghost."

"Mother believes in ghosts. But she wouldn't want one in our house."

Her house. She glanced toward the window and caught her breath. Horses. Carriages. Women held long skirts with bustles on the back out of the mud. Lord almighty, this was as real as could be. She didn't travel halfway this time—she'd gone the full distance into the past. A horse nickered from the street below, as though to punctuate this thought.

"I became dizzy…and fell."

The girl drew nearer. "I haven't seen you before, and your clothes are odd. If you're not a ghost, are you new?" Her tone grew impatient, obviously not accustomed to being ignored.

She stuttered out a response. "Y…yes, very new. My first day, in fact. I should go." *Before an adult discovers me here, in their house.*

As though the notion conjured someone, footsteps thumped on the stairs. Jillian swallowed a lump. Perhaps she had become a ghost, killed in an earthquake at some future time, and no one but this little girl could see her. If not, however, someone else might have more probing questions about her sudden presence, a stranger in their private residence. She closed her eyes, willing herself back to the present. Whatever this was that just happened wasn't good. She didn't belong here.

The girl wrinkled her nose. "March won't let you go around in that dress. Weren't you assigned a uniform?"

This was all a mistake. If a spirit summoned her to the past, they needed to release her. They were supposed to come to her, in her own time period. She didn't make house calls.

A tall woman dressed in black appeared in the doorway, staring down her hawk-like nose. Her high-necked dress had long sleeves and skirts that brushed the floor. "What is this? Who are you?"

Jillian's breath caught in her throat.

"Don't be frightened," the girl whispered in a kind tone. "Let me handle this." She faced the other woman and spoke with all the aplomb of an adult. "March, this is another one of mother's projects. See she gets a proper uniform."

The woman drew back her shoulders. "No one told me of a new girl."

"Mother's busy tending to Father. She can't consult with the housekeeper on every new maid she finds on the way home from church."

March sighed, a sound of one who found need to sigh often. "Where does she find them all?" she murmured and then gestured to Jillian. "Come with me, before anyone sees you. The family will come in for dinner soon." The woman focused on the girl. "Amy, I'm sure you'll be missed in the nursery. Run along and I'll find an outfit suitable for this new maid."

Maid.

Jillian didn't want to leave her spot by the window, the place that connected her to the present. She touched the window frame, solid under her fingers. A quick glance outside confirmed dirt streets and horses. This couldn't be happening.

"Hurry up, now." March's tone sharpened. "Whoever brought you to the family area? That boy, I imagine. Another of Mrs. Crocker's projects. She'll turn this place into an almshouse. And with three children of her own still to raise."

As though in a dream, Jillian followed the woman, in disbelief at the changed surroundings. The same house yet completely different. Now a fully furnished home, not a museum. Ornately carved walnut tables inlaid with rosewood, a set of Tiffany lamps, opulent tapestries, straight-backed chairs with embroidered seats. She quelled her panic as the housekeeper led her to where the long hallway had been. Now an arched doorway opened into an older structure, with creaking floors and windows that permitted a glimpse toward a changed world.

"This is the original mansion on the property," Mrs. March explained. "The Crockers built a more suitable home and now this part of their estate is used for staff. The kitchens are below. Your room will be upstairs. No one informed me of your arrival, so nothing is prepared."

What year *was* this? March's steady litany of complaints droned on in a murmur as they wound their way up a set of narrow stairs.

"You'll have to make do with this." March pushed open a door to reveal a small space, somewhat larger than a walk-in closet. "I'll get one of Sarah's uniforms, you'll have to take it in at the waist and lower the hem. You have no possessions?" The woman frowned as she scanned Jillian from head to toe. "What peculiar attire. Poor lamb."

Jillian shook her head and, remembering, clutched at an empty pocket. She must have dropped the cell phone in the earthquake. Laughter bubbled in her throat. What good would a cell phone do here? Who would answer the call? Perhaps a ceiling beam had hit her head in the quake, and she'd fallen into a fugue state. What if her body lay damaged and near death while her spirit wandered into a different century?

"You can start by sweeping this room. It's been closed up for nearly a year. I'll have the boy fetch up a cot." Mrs. March pursed her lips. "We're not an orphanage. Mrs. Crocker simply has to stop rescuing stray cats."

Once the housekeeper disappeared from sight, her multiple complaints trailing in her wake, Jillian dashed to the window. Her throat tightened at the panoramic view. The Sacramento from an hour ago no longer existed. In its place, where high rises once soared, lay a flat terrain. No levees constrained the wide Sacramento River. Low-slung buildings, some wooden and others brick, were under construction. To the north, with little else than a handful of trees in the way, she just made out the domed capitol building, scaffolding attached to one uncompleted side.

"The thirty-first state," she murmured, as she fought to recall history lessons from elementary school. California became a state in 1850, and the capitol city not decided upon until sometime later. But what year was this exactly? She couldn't ask the stiff and disapproving housekeeper.

"Hullo then."

A boy's voice behind her made her whirl. Skinny as a rail, he wore short tan pants that buttoned just below the knee, and an off-white long-sleeved shirt. He carried a thin folding cot. "It'll be hot as the devil in here in the summer but don't open the window. The mosquitoes will eat you alive." His eyes studied her and then, at the echo of footsteps, gave a wry grin. "That is, if March doesn't eat you alive first."

The boy saw her, too; she couldn't be a rootless spirit, detached from her body. She pinched the inside of her arm and winced. Not a dream. The boy unfolded the cot against one wall and darted out the door just as the housekeeper swept in, carrying a neat stack of clothing.

"I won't ask where she found you," March said, "but you have to dress decent and cover your arms and ankles if you are going to live here. This is a God-fearing household with impressionable young girls. Do not take advantage of Mrs. Crocker's good nature or you will answer to me." Jillian nodded her assent. "Do not bother the family and—" the housekeeper's eyes darkened. "—Do *not* speak to Mr. Crocker. He is a busy man and not well these days. If you need anything, talk to me."

Jillian bobbed her head in submission, her mouth too dry to speak and her tongue numb. A thousand questions raced through her mind but none were appropriate for the moment. At the top of the list: *Why am I here* and *how do I return*?

"You don't talk much though," March continued,

18

"so that's in your favor. Get on now. Change your clothes then sweep and tidy this room. There is a broom in the corner there, close enough it could've bit you. I will fetch you after the family has dined." Without waiting for a reply, the woman placed the uniform on the cot and departed. Her skirts stirred a fine layer of dust on the floor as she went.

Jillian sank onto the cot. She needed to get a grip. People called her talent of reaching into other worlds a gift. More than anything, she wished this gift had a return policy.

****

She dressed hurriedly to cover herself, her modern lace panties and bra sure to raise eyebrows and perhaps even mark her as a prostitute in earlier times. Fortunately, she had worn a long peasant skirt that day and not capris or an above-the-knee dress. The maid uniform consisted of a dark gray skirt with identical bodice and white apron. The ensemble fit large at the waist and bust. The long sleeves were oppressive in the heat of the May afternoon, especially in the confined third-floor space. She longed to roll the sleeves up to her elbows and unbutton the top few buttons of her shirtwaist, but she recalled the housekeeper's requirement to keep her arms covered. How did women survive the summer in climates like this?

"Still short but presentable," March declared when she returned, eying the hem which brushed the bottoms of Jillian's ankles. "It must do until I speak with Mrs. Crocker about you. We'll find you some sensible shoes. Heavens but you have big feet."

Jillian lowered her eyes at the mention of her supposed benefactress. As soon as March spoke to the woman, the authorities would be summoned and…she couldn't guess what might happen next. She needed to figure something out, but in the meantime, this was a safe haven. She had no money, no home, and no idea how to return to her own millennium.

"You can sweep the cobwebs from the ceiling later." The housekeeper frowned at the network of webs shrouding the corners. "I see you will need guidance in how to properly tidy a room. Best we start you in the scullery."

March led her down a set of narrow servants' stairs, hidden behind a wall, to the kitchen on the first floor. The housekeeper recited instructions and rules as they descended. She must be obedient and demure in behavior. Ten hours a day, six days a week, three Sundays a month off. Today, her first Sunday on duty, counted as a workday though nearly over. In return for her labors, she'd receive room and board, and two dollars a week. Jillian listened in horror at the paltry salary, though generous according to March.

"Mrs. Stevens will be glad of the help," the housekeeper said by way of introduction to the cook, who arranged thin slices of cake on crystal dishes.

"Only don't bother me now," the other woman said, perspiration at her brow. "I'm in the middle of service. The ices didn't freeze, and now I have to send up yesterday's cake. It will have to do, though the girls will be disappointed."

"Not a problem, Mrs. Stevens; I'll set her to work. Never fear, the family will love your cake."

Jillian's stomach rumbled, reminding her it had been hours since she'd eaten. Mrs. March, however, steered her toward a sink trough in the scullery, apparently her new workplace. A grim exchange for her usual laptop and desk.

The boy who had toted her cot upstairs scooted past, arms heaped with wood. "Getting your 'Marching' orders yet?" he whispered with a wink.

"I noticed the front steps need to be scrubbed." March's haughty nose rose higher. "Do that next, Caleb."

"I swear, Mrs. March, you have eyes on the back of your head," the boy quipped.

"Best think twice before you speak."

Caleb filled the wood box by the kitchen stove and scurried off. The housekeeper kept a sharp eye on the boy until the door shut behind him. "What is your name, girl; I didn't ask and you are as quiet as the grave."

"Jillian."

The woman grimaced and shook her head. "Absurd. Whatever happened to solid Christian names? We'll call you Jane." March didn't wait for assent but pointed to the sink. "Supper dishes need to be washed; mind you don't chip the china. Shipped all the way from Germany, can you imagine?"

Somehow she needed some questions answered. Screwing up her courage, Jillian rounded on the woman. "Mrs. March, I-I hate to…"

"Another time, my dear. I've work to do." The housekeeper strode out of the scullery without a backward glance.

Through the open doorway that connected the scullery to the kitchen, Mrs. Stevens chortled over her cakes. "She's a tough old carrot, but soft as pudding inside. Do your work, say your prayers, and everything will work out well."

A young maid, in an outfit that matched her own, stepped into the kitchen. Her eyes grew wide when she saw Jillian. "A new one. No one said."

"Hurry, girl, get these cakes upstairs."

The other maid set the glass plates on a tray, darted another curious glance her direction, and rushed away. Jillian faced the sink trough, stacked with a heap of food-crusted dishes and pans. A long handle rose from the side and she lifted it to turn on the water only to find nothing happened. Glancing toward the cook, who bustled around a long table, Jillian lowered and lifted the handle again.

"Heavens, put some muscle into it," the cook said, suddenly at her elbow with a bucket of hot water. "We use hot water for dishes in this house, not just the cold. Refill the bucket when you're done and set it on the stove."

A pump! She heaved at the handle, relieved to see the water flow. Modern plumbing, electricity, cars, airplanes, telephones—all gone, part of a time yet to occur. A wave of dizziness made her lightheaded. Maybe she'd gone mad. She gripped the edge of the sink, solid and cool beneath her fingers.

The basin steamed as the hot water mixed with the cold and perspiration beaded on her forehead. She set to work on the dishes with a square of lye soap before March returned and another scolding landed on her head. The lye soap stung her hands and the hot water burned; too real to be a dream.

One step at a time, she reminded herself. She'd faced difficult situations before. There had to be a way out of this predicament.

Any moment, she'd be whisked back to her own time. Comforted with that reflection, she scraped and scrubbed, rinsed and dried.

Any moment.

Chapter Three

"My mother and brother died years ago, in a car, uh, carriage accident," Jillian explained over a dinner of chicken, turnips, gravy, and crusty bread.

With more than a dozen people crowded shoulder to shoulder around the table, the servants' dining hall felt cramped and stuffy. Two small windows high on the wall allowed light in but only the barest of breezes. Introductions flew around the table and her still-reeling mind forgot most of their names as soon as they were uttered. Occupations stuck better—stable boys, head gardener, maids. More staff worked at the residence, she learned, but the others had gone home for their dinner.

All eyes fixed on her as she sought to weave a plausible tale. "My father and I lived near San Francisco, but I haven't seen him in months." The words were true, as she'd lived in her own cottage in Mendocino, north of the Golden Gate city, since the age of twenty-four.

"And what brought you to Sacramento?" One of the other maids, somewhere in her mid-twenties with a pile of dark hair twisted into a tight heap atop her head, tore off a chunk of bread from the plate and glanced at Caleb. "And upon hard times. I mean, no clothes or personal effects with you. Did you escape a wicked husband?"

March shot the young woman a warning look. "We don't talk of such evils over the Lord's table."

"I just asked what we all want to know," the maid said, her tone sulky.

Forks clinked against plates, but no one else spoke. Eyebrows raised expectantly as the other staff members at the table waited to hear the rest of Jillian's tale of misfortune and woe. Her mind raced to create a credible story to relate.

"I'm not married," she said hurriedly, then had an inspiration. "Yet. I came seeking my, uh, intended. He traveled to the gold fields months ago and I'm afraid he's come to some harm." As she spoke, she recalled the museum painting that captured Mason's image in such fine detail. But he traveled to Brazil, not Northern California, not anywhere close. This *must* be some strange dream, born of raw oysters and pickled kimchee, the combination so surprisingly delicious the night before.

"A common story, I'm afraid," March said, with a tsk of her tongue. "Too many men and not enough gold to satisfy them. They fall into uncivilized habits and iniquity."

"He could have been set upon by robbers and buried in a shallow grave," Caleb offered to a round of shushing.

Jillian gazed around the table to continue her pretense of a woman in search of a truant fiancé. "How can I go about finding someone?"

March shook her head. "You should have stayed home and waited. This is no place for a woman alone."

"You're the one who needed rescuing," the dark-haired maid added.

Jillian tucked her head to study the table. A sheen of grease floated over the remnants of brown gravy on the plate. Her brain seemed frozen and thawed much too slowly to deal with this situation. But—better to be pitied than questioned further.

"Leave the girl alone, Sarah," said the estate's gardener—Zeb, she recalled—a husky man in his forties. "Can't you see she's suffered? Where's your Christian kindness?"

Sarah set down her fork with a clatter. "Jane's taken my spare uniform and now I have to wear this one an extra day. You try to serve table for two little girls and stay tidy."

Jillian blinked at the usage of her new name. A sense of unreality swept through her again. The mention of the family's children reminded her of the girl she'd met earlier who called her a ghost. Her old life ebbed away bit by bit—her clothes, possessions, time, and now her name. How long before she winked out of existence altogether?

March cleared her throat and glared at the sulky maid. "Hush, girl. As though you ever had more than two dresses before you arrived at this house. We'll get it sorted once I speak with Mrs. Crocker."

Jillian poked at the chicken on her plate, chilled at the reference to their employer. She had no idea what reason she could offer as to how she, dressed in what must have appeared as a nightgown, ended up in the mansion. Perhaps the best course of action would be to sneak out that very night before her ruse was discovered.

The buzz of conversation droned around her as she pushed food about her plate and corralled her fear.

Silverware clinked against plates and Mrs. Stevens rose to refill the bread plate. The aroma of peach pies cooling in the adjacent kitchen wafted through the door.

"Jenny had the prettiest dress you ever saw at dinner tonight," said a petite somewhat cross-eyed maid in her late teens. "All flounces in the back and a tidy bow in her hair."

"Even though she's only twelve, she'll turn out to be the pride of the family, mark my words," Sarah added. "Can't say the same for Amy. I heard her shout at Miss Temple yesterday."

Jillian frowned and peered at the other faces, the household names which flew by too quickly for her to grasp. Caleb met her puzzled look and rolled his eyes. "Miss Temple's an unfortunate one all right. She's Amy's nanny. Eats alone in the schoolroom."

"Too good for some of us, not good enough for others," Zeb said in a wise tone.

"There are two older daughters, as well," Caleb said, leaning toward Jillian. "I expect they'll marry fine gentlemen soon."

"A house full of daughters." Zeb chimed in. "Poor Mr. Crocker."

"Nothing poor about this family," Sarah said with a sniff. "They built an entire building to show off their artwork, with the entire first floor a ballroom. This estate is even bigger than Mr. Leland Stanford's, even after the recent additions."

"Raised the whole house twelve feet, Mr. Stanford did, because of the floods the year he was elected governor," Zeb said with a chuckle. "Had to take a rowboat to be sworn in."

March tapped her knife against the wooden table

and the conversation died. She redirected talk with the skill of one used to a mutinous crew. "The painting arrives tomorrow, so everyone will take special care to look sharp. Mr. Crocker will be down early to supervise the placement. I don't want a hair out of place."

Caleb spoke through a mouthful of turnips. "I hear there are gamblers and robbers in this one. I can't wait."

"And men reading the Bible," the gardener added in a firm voice. "Not only sinners."

"But Mr. Crocker specifically asked for sinful activities," Caleb insisted. "That's what I heard."

"Your ears need to be cleaned," Sarah said, and glanced at March for confirmation. "Mr. Crocker would never request evil deeds be put in a picture."

Sinners. Men reading the Bible. This could be no coincidence. "What is this picture?"

"A very famous German painter has created a piece at Mr. Crocker's behest," March said. "The portrayal is called 'Sunday Morning in the Mines.' "

Jillian bit back a gasp. *1872,* the year the museum guard told her this very piece was completed. Her heart raced. Even though the table sat firmly in front of her and the aroma of fresh bread and savory gravy filled her senses, the reality of her situation remained difficult to absorb. But knowing the date somehow made circumstances tangible. And one of the men within this very painting bore an incredible likeness to Mason. Her intuition screamed that the picture had something to do with her journey into the past. Her Aussie boyfriend didn't have a single ghost-hunting sinew in his body— and the possibility a spirit or some other supernatural force trapped him also in 1872 defied belief.

"Jane." Mrs. Stevens' tone startled Jillian. The

cook's disapproving stare settled upon her uneaten dinner.

"We don't waste good food in this house," the cook said, her tone laced with peevishness. "We eat what we have been fortunate enough to receive. I doubt you've enjoyed such a fine meal in quite some time."

She picked up her fork in a hurry. "Yes, ma'am. I- it's just that I'm a bit overcome with everyone's kindness. Being here today…this is a different world for me." *You have no idea.*

"Eat your food, girl," Mrs. March said. "You'll feel right at home after a good night's rest."

****

A round of goodnights followed dinner. March, Caleb, the two other maids, and Jillian slept in the servants' quarters in the house; the stable boys had rooms in the stable. She had learned the servants housed on the property, all except for March, were Mrs. Crocker's "projects," the term used for rescued street waifs, as the household believed her to be.

After washing another round of dishes, Jillian climbed the servants' stairs to her tiny quarters, grateful for time alone to consider her options. She'd read theoretical arguments that time travel could be possible, but of course, this was one theory no one had ever proven. On her cot, she studied a deep cut on one finger from the hefty butcher knife that hid beneath a pot in the kitchen basin. The blood had been very real and the gash still smarted. Survival instinct warned her no antibiotics yet existed if an infection set in. She had cleaned the cut several times, the astringent soap so strong it brought tears to her eyes.

She peered around the bare room and yearned for a

notepad. For two decades, from the age of eight, she'd scribbled bits and thoughts each day, first as a diary and then a blog. In her late teens, her Spirited Quest blog evolved into a successful online business. The urge to write down this unbelievable day's events made her fingers itch for a laptop, a phone, even a scrap of paper and pencil.

Dear readers, she murmured. *This time a quest is not of my own design. I've tumbled headlong into the year 1872 and...*

For the first time, words deserted her. The events defied description. She rose, stripped off the white apron, gray dress, petticoats, and black stockings, and let the heavy pile of clothing drop to the floor in a heap. In her bra and panties, the only apparel she had that belonged to her own time, she felt more herself. Jillian Winchester, successful businesswoman, instead of Jane the maid with no last name and a fictional past.

Despite Caleb's warnings about mosquitoes, she opened the window and gazed out into the darkened city. No electric streetlights, just a few dull glows from gas lit lamps from the direction of the unfinished capitol and a few by the river. The stars, however, gleamed more brilliant than she'd ever seen, unsullied by manmade illumination. These are the same stars as the ones in my time, she comforted herself. To the stars, a hundred and fifty years was a blink of the eye.

She needed to study the miners' camp painting once more for clues. There had to be a reason for this twist of nature that sent her into the past. The concept that this was a freak accident of the cosmos, with no key to a return journey, overwhelmed her senses. She pulled on the scratchy calico nightgown left on her cot.

A matching night cap she hurled in a corner in defiance. So many clothes and on such a warm night! The act of rebellion cheered her somewhat.

The cot squeaked as she lay down; the linens lacked the softness of modern fabrics. Her mind drifted to the events that brought her to this specific era. Why here? Why now? The 1920s' flapper era would have been fun, the sixties hippie decade enlightening, the nineties—her eyes flew open. The nineties would have given her a chance to see her mother and brother again, before the crash killed and took them away from her forever. The 1870s, though, were darned uncomfortable. Complaints flooded her mind, as she resettled her head on the lumpy pillow.

Change your situation or change your attitude. Sometimes you must do the second to achieve the first.

These were words she'd read once, good advice that served her well. She'd landed in a mansion, clothed and fed, and with a job. A bed, sheets, and blanket. A room with a view. Keep it simple, she ordered herself, and *think*. Something must have triggered this event. Her journey to the past started with what felt like an earthquake. She'd been in the Crocker mansion dining room. A guard hovered nearby. There had been the Asian man who appeared to her twice, once in the window and again right before the quake.

Could a spirit drag her into the past? And, if so, why didn't he appear to her now?

It wasn't as though she'd stroked an ancient lamp or touched a relic. She'd just been on the phone to contact…

Mason.

The man in the painting—the same one that would

arrive tomorrow—was the very image of Mason. The picture's likeness of him and her inability to contact him had to be related. Had Mason also been transported to 1872? She had seen him, spoken to him, touched him, less than twenty-four hours ago, not enough time for an artist to capture his likeness in a commissioned piece of art.

Frustrated, she closed her eyes and reviewed the scene in the dining room. The guard, the spirit, the phone, the earthquake. When the temblor stopped, her sudden appearance frightened a little girl into believing she was a ghost. Although…the Crockers' youngest child, Amy, hadn't been alarmed at all…almost as though she'd seen others come and go. Amy might know something helpful.

Somehow, she needed to speak with the child, inspect the painting again, and avoid Mrs. Crocker's notice. She had to keep her eyes open for the spirit; he must live or work nearby in these times. Then she would find a way home. Comforted with a plan and exhausted by the day, Jillian fell into a deep slumber.

Chapter Four

An outraged voice startled Jillian awake to find that light streamed through the window. Hands fisted on narrow hips, March loomed like a huge black crow. "How dare you?"

Jillian shoved off the covers in a rush and scooted from the bed to stand in her bare feet. Still 1872. This bad dream-that-was-not-a-dream persisted. And the nightmare named March scowled, as real as a slap in the face.

The housekeeper's face glowered, red and furious. The ruse was up. The police might arrive any minute and lock her in jail, perhaps prison, stuck in the past forever. Unless they executed imposters, thieves, and fraudsters. Heaven help her.

March pointed to the crumpled heap of clothing in the middle of the room, her voice filled with contained fury. "This is how you treat the kindness and decency of our employer. You'd think a wardrobe filled with fine gowns stood in the corner, and a lady's maid waited to launder and iron your belongings."

The rebuke continued. "Caleb will have you to thank for the dishes he now has to wash while you iron your uniform. If this was up to me, you'd be out on the street. I will certainly let Mrs. Crocker know of this behavior. You are fortunate she is busy with Mr. Crocker, getting him ready for the new artwork to arrive. I *will* bring this to her attention later today."

Jillian's knees grew weak with relief. Discovery of her deception appeared to be delayed a bit longer. She needed to stay in the house to determine if the image in the painting was truly Mason's. Then, locate the child. Prison didn't factor in her plans.

Instinct drove her to an impulsive act of self-preservation. She dropped to her knees before the housekeeper and gripped the hem of her black skirt. "Please, Mrs. March. I have nowhere to go. No family. Nothing but the undeserved kindness I've found here." The words rushed from her with the comprehension that the housekeeper held the keys to her future. "I was so overwhelmed by yesterday, and this is the first full night's sleep I've had since I left home. Give me another chance, and I won't let you down. I'll work twice as hard—"

Her heart drummed a staccato rhythm and she swallowed back a sudden terror of being thrown out to fend for herself.

"Hush, girl." March's tone softened and she laid a hand on Jillian's shoulder. "Heavens, you finally found your tongue. Get on your feet." The housekeeper tugged her skirt free and averted her gaze as though embarrassed by her newest maid's desperate entreaty. "No one's going to send you away. You are inexperienced and thoughtless, but I've trained worse. Now, gather your clothes and we'll get you on the right path soon enough." She huffed a sigh. "Mrs. Crocker is much too kind; too kind by far."

Jillian clambered to her feet, scooped up the uniform, and followed the woman to a room used for sewing and ironing. Fortunately, only the apron needed

34

serious attention.

Unfortunately, she was downstairs elbows deep in the sink basin within the hour.

****

Time lurched forward with one chore after another. Either March or Mrs. Stevens assigned the next task in a tag team manner that kept Jillian glancing over her shoulder in fear of one or the other's approach with yet another job for her to do. A furious burst of activity throughout the house alerted her to the arrival of the artwork. Steps sounded above the kitchen, where the corridor crossed from the mansion to the gallery building. March swept in and out of the kitchen with a frenzy, like a fretful raven, as though she alone managed the momentous occasion.

None of the household staff, in fact, took part in the painting's placement. Mr. Crocker had hired specialists in this regard, skilled in the careful handling of fine art at the proper location and height. March ensured staff didn't interrupt the procedure by traveling up the staircase or crossing the main hallway.

Stationed in the kitchen workroom, Jillian startled each time March burst through, fearful the inevitable conversation with their employer had occurred. When the housekeeper departed again, Jillian's focus returned to the artwork newly hung in the gallery, and she quelled a tremendous impulse to rush to the stairs and view the miners' camp scene once more. Of *course*, the man wasn't Mason. Her imagination had been working overtime. Still, a persistent voice inside contended she hadn't been mistaken, and this voice became more forceful as the morning wore on.

With a thunk, Mrs. Stevens dropped three dead

birds on the table where Jillian had spent the past hour, polishing an endless line of silver trays. "Three chickens," she barked. "I want them plucked clean. There'll be no pin feathers in Mrs. Crocker's mouth. Not from my kitchen."

Jillian gaped at the birds, who appeared to stare back from blank glassy eyes. A musty smell of henhouse and feathers swirled in the air. "Pluck?" she squeaked. "Here? How?"

The cook sighed and rested a beefy hand on the table. Strands of gray hair had slipped free and straggled at her neck. "My dear, did they not have chickens where you're from? They're just like any other fowl. Grab and pull. On the back step, and make sure you drape a towel across your lap first." The woman pointed at a large wooden bowl that hung on the wall. "Put them in there when you're done. Go on now, the silver will wait until you get back."

"Oh, good. I don't want to miss any of this." Jillian muttered.

Mrs. Stevens' lips curled up as she strolled back into the main kitchen. "Idle hands make devil's work."

Jillian lifted her hands and studied them with a jaundiced eye. "Did you hear that, guys? You're headed for sainthood." She scooted back her chair and grabbed the limp chickens. "Grab and pull," she muttered to herself. If nothing else, the work would occupy her until the hubbub around the painting quieted and she had a chance to slip away from chores to study the canvas again.

Outside, on the broad granite steps, for the first time outdoors since her arrival into the past, Jillian had an opportunity to breathe fresh air. All around were trees and dirt. No concrete or asphalt, and in this part of town, not even wooden walkways. The sky a deep sapphire, unblemished by a single cloud, and a soft aroma of sawn wood drifted on the air. Not far away lay the burgeoning capitol city; before her, some distance away, horses grazed in a field.

Behind the carriage house, the Sacramento River sprawled wide, slow-moving, and dark. Large river dams in this region wouldn't be built for another fifty years and this meant entire trees, dead animals, and all manner of debris tumbled through the waters. She'd always been a strong swimmer, since she lived her entire life by the Pacific Ocean. If catastrophe struck and the sheriff appeared, she could sprint for her life, throw herself on the mercy of the river, and strike out for the opposite shore. The muddy river, filled with hidden dangers, didn't appear promising. Hopefully, that option wouldn't become necessary.

Jillian settled down to her work, with a bucket between her knees and birds at her side. She wrinkled her nose at the unfamiliar task. "Grab and pull" transformed into "grab and rip," a horrifying sensation as feathers popped free from flesh. After a few minutes of work, the feathers flew under her hands, with bits of fluff escaping across the yard.

From time to time, she paused in her task to observe Zeb and Caleb hard at work on the grounds. They trimmed already neat shrubbery and weeded any tiny sprouts that dared invade pristine garden beds. Large swallowtail butterflies flitted past, and grasshoppers clicked their legs in the grass. Mrs. Stevens emerged from the kitchen twice to check on the progress of her fowl before she completed the task.

With chickens in the wooden bowl and a bucket of feathers, she returned to the scullery to discover calm had descended on the household. March was nowhere in sight and Mrs. Stevens had her hands and wrists buried in flour and dough. Now or never.

Jillian stole out of the kitchen and crept up the back stairs. She pressed an ear to the door to the main foyer. The earlier hubbub had faded, and now all had fallen silent. She took a deep breath and cracked open the door. All clear. She scooted down the corridor to the gallery building to view the grand staircase.

The massive artwork, looming high above the main hall, took her breath away. There it hung, the very same piece in the exact spot where she'd first seen it. From her spot at the base of the stairs, details blurred, too far to make out. Checking both directions, she left the safety of the doorway and edged closer. The picture now drew her forth like a magnet, up to the first landing, her eyes riveted on the scene as she scanned it for Mason's image.

There. Just as before. No, even more definite. The man with his fist raised was without a doubt her Aussie boyfriend. This was no double. The way his hair curled when it grew too long, the slight twist at the side of his mouth when he focused on a difficult problem. Even captured in a painting, his very-real image evoked desire in her core. She took a step closer and craned her neck at the artwork.

Now below the canvas, engrossed and mouth slightly agape, she studied the picture for any clues to this incomprehensible situation. The air escaped her mouth in a rush, as if someone squeezed her lungs in an iron grip. A second man, on the right third of the picture…it couldn't be…was also Mason. Even in part profile, he was recognizable. This version of him sat just inside an open cabin door, the man hunched over a desk who appeared to write a letter. Both the sins and virtues in a mining camp, illustrated within this painting, and Mason's image represented both. Her mind worked furiously to figure out what this meant.

"Do you like my latest acquisition?"

Jillian jumped back with a start. A white-haired man with a chest-length beard stood just below her, pale gray eyes kind and gentle. This was a face she'd seen in portraiture when this mansion was a museum just a day earlier, one hundred and fifty years in the future, long after his demise. The merging of past and future prompted a sense of vertigo.

Mr. Crocker's gaze lifted to the canvas. "As well you should. This one's a masterpiece."

Mrs. March had warned over and over never to speak to Mr. Crocker. But this painting, with its mysterious double depiction of Mason, demanded she speak. "I nearly feel as though I'm there in one of the camps," she ventured. "The imagery is so real, the colors quite vivid."

The great man's face broke into a delighted smile, and he climbed the final few steps to stand at her side. "Just so." He swept one hand across, from one edge of the frame to the other. "You view the divisive nature of men, and how the mighty lure of immorality strives to overwhelm the best resolve."

Her attention darted from the respectable Mason on the right to his wayward twin on the left. "I noticed an intriguing feature." She gestured toward the two depictions. "This man appears to be the same person."

Her words elicited a deep chuckle from her employer. "You have the eye of an art critic, my dear. Inspect even closer and you'll see there are others with a double. Man is a complicated creature and one of two natures. The artist, Charles Nahl, makes this point, but in a subtle manner." His pale eyes studied her with more interest. "Not everyone notices this particular detail. Bravo, young lady."

"How wonderful." She hesitated before she continued. "And the models he used must have spent a fair amount of time in a studio. Where might Mr. Nahl obtain them? The models, I mean."

His eyes crinkled in amusement as he plucked a chicken feather from her shoulder. A slight medicinal scent drifted her way. A gray tinge lay under his skin, and his jowls sagged loosely. "I never considered these might be real people. I suppose an artist must have his archetypes."

Not wanting to appear too anxious on this point, she shifted her gaze to the mining scene and waited. Mason *here*, in Sacramento. Or, at least, he had been here. Her heart thudded in her chest, and a pulse drummed in her ears.

"Mr. Nahl has a studio in town." Mr. Crocker stroked his beard. "You may very well run into one of the men in the painting as you take an afternoon stroll." He chuckled. "I do hope you meet him engaged in the right behavior and—" He nodded to the other side of the artwork. "—not the left."

A soft cough drew Jillian's attention to the bottom of the stairs where a stormy-faced March stared at her. "Excuse me, sir," the housekeeper said through thinned lips. "Jane escaped my notice. I do apologize." Her tone turned icy. "Come with me *now*, Jane."

"It's never a bother to chat with a lovely young woman." His eyes twinkled before his mouth settled into a frown, and deep lines grooved his forehead. "Go easy on the girl, Mrs. March."

Jillian descended the stairs with her gaze focused on her feet. Step one—to confirm Mason's image in the painting—was complete. Step two—speak to the little girl, Amy, to determine if Mason had also traveled through this house. Then she would locate Mr. Nahl's studio. At the moment, she needed to defuse the ticking bomb at the bottom of the stairs.

"Into the scullery," March hissed from the side of her mouth as soon as Jillian's foot touched the main floor. "Your apron has *blood* on it."

"Yes, ma'am."

By the front door, a clock chimed the hour. The echo of the chimes followed Jillian as she followed the housekeeper to the kitchen. Eleven a.m. No more than twenty-four hours since the earthquake, or whatever it had been, and she'd fallen back in time. Working as a maid under a dictator like March made it seem much longer.

****

"Mr. Crocker is terribly ill." March didn't hide the tremor in her voice. "He is not to be weighed down with the trivial chatter of household maids."

This was so unfair. Even though March warned her to stay clear of family areas, Jillian never started the conversation. She met the housekeeper's stare. "He approached *me*. Should I have ignored him?"

"You excuse yourself quickly and not stand there, jabbering away like a monkey," came the all too quick snapped response. March's shoulders sagged, a sudden movement that appeared to drag her cheeks downward as well. "Jane, Jane, what am I to do with you? I've yet to encounter a more insubordinate girl. I do wonder if you're more suited for a different path in this world."

For the first time, Jillian wondered what kind of life Mrs. March lived. Had there once been a Mr. March? The woman had to be at least fifty. What might happen to a woman in her station of life when she grew too old to work, in these pre-Social Security days? Apparently, no home of her own. Perhaps there was kin—a sister or brother—who waited to take her in.

"I promise you won't have any more trouble from me," she vowed, and fought to not cross her fingers like a child from the lie. If all went well, she meant to vanish without a trace once she located Mason and discovered a way to return to their own time.

"You have had your final warning. Mrs. Crocker will see me at three this afternoon. I will let her know I've gotten you situated comfortably and suggest that your...well...natural talents may not be suited for this household." March straightened and her jaw firmed. "I will not recommend your dismissal. Yet."

"Yes, ma'am." Before the woman went on to assign a new round of duties, Jillian raced on. "Mrs. March, a quick question. Are there any Asian employees here?"

The woman's brow furrowed. "Asian? I suppose you mean Chinese? What an odd question. But no, not at the moment, though the Crockers aren't against them as many are. I hope you don't hold a hostile attitude. Mr. Crocker is a famous abolitionist and won't tolerate prejudice in any form."

She shook her head. "Nothing of the kind. There is a man who I believe may have information about my fiancé."

"There are more than fifteen thousand people in Sacramento. It's gotten so crowded one can hardly move about these days. To locate one man will be like searching for a needle in a haystack."

The information lifted her spirits. Fifteen thousand was a small town. A far cry from the future metropolis with more than two million people. "I traveled a long way and am determined to bring my fiancé home. Is it possible for me to go into town today to make inquiries? I'd be quick and return right away. I'd work extra." Again, a lie. At three p.m., when the housekeeper spoke to Mrs. Crocker, her deception would be laid bare. She had to find Mason by then. If the Crocker mansion was key to their return to the present, they needed access to the house. And Amy…she must speak with the girl. Time was fleeting.

The housekeeper's eyes widened before they narrowed. Any softness in her earlier expression disappeared. "Absolutely not. You receive Sundays off. Not whenever you'd like." She shook her head as she stalked away. "A different path in life, I warrant. That is what lies ahead for you." Without a pause in her step, the woman called over her shoulder, "Clean your apron, then the feathers from the back step. Work to do, girl."

Jillian untied her apron and studied the smear of blood at her waist. "I do hope there's a different path for me," she murmured.

Taking a deep breath, she set her apron on a chair and headed out the back door. Feathers drifted on the lightest of breezes, escapees from her labors. The fluffs and quills tumbled end over end across the yard as though a chicken had exploded there. The late morning sun streamed against her face and shoulders. From the direction of the city's central district sounded the sharp echoes of hammers on wood and the ring of metal tools against stone, as though all of Sacramento underwent construction at once

Mason. Somewhere amidst the construction, he existed, met Mr. Nahl the artist, and ended up in a very famous painting. As crazy as this seemed, they were both here in 1872. She needed to find him.

Once her feet started to inch forward, they wouldn't stop. She crossed the yard as fast as her skirts allowed. Talking to the little girl was trivial compared to finding Mason. March would never let her back in the Crocker mansion now. There was no turning back.

Chapter Five

Doubts tumbled in and slowed her pace. She had made a mistake in leaving the Crocker mansion. She had no money. Her plan had been to talk to Amy first. Each fact chipped away at the confidence she'd had just moments ago. But the possibility of Mason being somewhere in the city, lost in time like her, propelled her forward. A selfish part of her wished he was there to share in this bizarre turn of events; an equal part hoped otherwise.

As she neared town, she took in the scene. Her earlier impression of an entire city under construction wasn't far off the mark. Men with shovels packed dirt onto streets, and carts hauled bricks up to half-finished structures. Dust, the stench of horse droppings, and shouts of laborers filled the air. Ceaseless activity buzzed everywhere, just as busy as any modern-day city, as though a critical deadline neared for completion. But this wasn't just any city; this was 1872 and the landscape far different from what existed in contemporary times.

She rolled her hands into fists, determined not to let fear win out. People remained people, no matter what century. Thanks to her drab gray dress, plaited hair now twisted into a chignon at the nape of her neck, and not a trace of makeup, no one gave her a second glance. By outward appearances she belonged, not as strange a creature as a woman from Venus might be.

"Watch it!" A middle-aged woman in a doorway flashed her an angry grimace as she almost splashed a bucket of foul-smelling water on Jillian's skirts.

She skittered out of the way into the street directly in front of a mule-drawn cart.

"Oy!" A man yelled, from atop the cart. He simultaneously heaved back on the reins and turned the mule's head to one side. "You want to be killed?"

Heart racing, Jillian gathered her skirts so she wouldn't stumble and scooted off the road.

The woman in the doorway spat onto the street. "Irishmen." Her tone left no doubt as to how she felt about the cart's driver. She whirled and disappeared inside.

Jillian closed her eyes and breathed deep for a count of five. More than ever, she needed to keep her wits about her. Stay in the moment, she counseled herself. Stay alert.

She hurried onward, not quite sure where to begin the search for Mr. Nahl's studio. An artist of his prestige must be located in one of the nicer buildings—somewhere Mr. Crocker would be apt to visit. Realizing her quick pace drew attention, she slowed to a stroll and forced herself to inhale with slow breaths.

The capitol now in sight, Jillian angled toward it in fascination. From the time she was a child, this structure was as familiar as any government building in the country. Now, the state's capitol appeared almost unrecognizable. The wide grassy park that surrounded the structure had freshly planted saplings and not the giant oaks, magnolias, and cedars of the future. More dramatic was the abbreviated size of the structure. An entire wing didn't exist, along with the fountain and great seal that adorned a sidewalk, nor any sidewalks at all. More than any other transformation, however— what made her stop in her tracks—were the cattle that grazed on the lawn and open land beyond where dense neighborhoods would one day sprout. No high-rises, or smog from automobile exhaust, blocked a crystal-clear view of the Sierra Nevada mountain range that rose in the distance. In a hundred and fifty years, the city climbed well into the foothills to the east, a messy sprawl of houses and businesses, and the view of the mountains lost to a permanent urban haze.

A lump stuck in her throat as she faced away from the state's seat of government. This land sat on the verge of wilderness, newly won from Mexico and long believed to be uninhabitable swampy terrain. Before her now, to the west, burgeoned a nascent metropolis. Beyond the river to the west, now mostly unsettled land, density and traffic would thicken all the way to the Bay Area and Pacific Ocean. Semi-trucks would roar past with loads of cattle and tomatoes, the air rife with car horns and ambulance sirens.

Her focus needed to remain on her task or panic over the disparities between present and future might escalate and paralyze her into inaction. She must find Mason. Together, they would figure out a way to escape this unfamiliar place and time. To believe herself vulnerable or trapped here forever was not an option. This improbable occurrence still made her dizzy. How could a trip into the past happen? Why her and Mason?

The assault of questions in her mind clamored, eroding her confidence each time she shored it up.

What if we're dead?

This was no more far-fetched than time travel. No one truly knew what happened after death. Perhaps souls, once untethered from the world, voyaged through time. Even more reason to find Mason. If they were dead... *Stop*, she ordered herself. *Focus*.

Another few deep breaths later, and her composure returned. She set off toward downtown, quelling the urge to gawk at every peculiar difference. Women's bodies neatly molded by corsets into dresses, and nearly all men wore vests and hats, like actors on a detailed set. She concentrated instead on signs above the shops and businesses that lined the street. The store names were in a bygone language: draper, haberdashery, milliner.

"I'd pay well for the golden locks upon your head." A man stood in a doorway of a barber shop and eyed her hair with the sharp gaze of a professional. "A fine head of hair and one that should be shared." He beckoned toward his door. "Come inside and you'll be a gold piece richer in no time. A fair trade, gold for gold."

Jillian edged away from the doorway, but recalling the near miss that occurred earlier, stayed on the wooden walkway. "No thank you. Another time perhaps." She fingered her hair at the nape. How desperate might the next days be? Would she return to this barber to peddle her locks?

The pungent aroma of horse manure assaulted her anew, and a quick glance street-ward explained why. With so many animals used for transportation and haulage, summer in the city would reek. Ahead, two wagons were tied up in front of a brick building with a large sign declaring it a general store. Even a famous artist needed groceries. Jillian left the barber behind and opened the heavy wooden door.

"…made up for lost time and ruined goods." A thick-set man with an outsized black beard and sideburns spoke from behind the counter. He wore a tan apron tied around his generous middle.

A woman in a straw bonnet tied under her chin with a yellow ribbon gathered up paper-wrapped packages and gave him a nod. "I'd never believe it if I didn't see it for myself. To cart in enough dirt to lift the streets by an entire story. Now we enter your establishment through what used to be a window on the second level. Makes me feel quite daring."

"It took a bit of dirt and effort, but from now on, my merchandise will be safe from the spring floods," the large man said. "And your feet shall stay dry." He tucked a spare piece of twine below the counter and gazed expectantly at Jillian as the woman left. "Here for an order, miss?"

A handful of customers browsed the shelves, most of them women, although she saw one sour-faced man lurking nearby.

"Actually, I'm searching for someone. Well, a couple of people. Have you met a man named Mason?"

The shop owner stroked his beard. "No one who identified himself as such. A brother or husband?"

"My intended. His speech sounds, well, from England." This was easier than explaining Australia belonged to the British Empire; at least, she thought this true in 1872.

The man who loitered nearby laid his selections on the counter with a sneer. "My great-grandfather shot a

Brit, back in the Battle of Yorktown. General Washington himself gave him a medal. Proudest moment in our family."

"I'm speaking to the lady, Hoke," the shop owner said, in a tone that implied he knew the other man well and didn't like him. "You can tell your story later."

Jillian glanced between the two men. "Or perhaps a Mr. Nahl. I understand he's a famous artist."

To her relief, the store proprietor nodded. "I know the German. Used to order sausage every week without fail but haven't seen him of late."

"Don't think any of my kinfolk ever shot a German," the other man broke in. "Have we ever quarreled with them?"

Jillian's hopes rose on the store owner's reply. "Do you know where I might find him? I've been told he has a studio here in town."

"You've been told right. His studio is on the street over yonder. the tall, wooden building. It is one of the few original structures that didn't burn down in the last big fire."

The other man thumped a fist on the counter. "Too many foreigners land here every day. They should stay home before they get shot, one and all."

Jillian couldn't help herself. Prejudice was prejudice, no matter what century. "And what country are your ancestors from?" she asked in a honeyed tone.

The man's face darkened further. "An American-speaking one." He gripped his supplies tight to his chest and headed to the door. "Put this on my account."

The store owner chuckled behind her, his voice deep and hearty. "Well said, my dear. We're all from somewhere else, aren't we now. My parents were born in Ohio, but theirs came from England. My grandfather spoke the King's English, with an accent to match." He grabbed a book from below the counter and scribbled a few notes. "Hoke's account is as long as my arm. Only reason I put up with him is on account of him being my wife's second cousin."

For the first time that day, she relaxed. A pleasant face and kindly tone went a long way. "Next street over, you said?"

"Yes, ma'am." The store owner set a lemon drop candy on the counter. "Have a sweet, no charge. Worth it to see Hoke put in his place."

****

There was no mistaking the tall wooden building, although tall meant three stories, for every other structure consisted of brick. No signage outside, however, indicated an artist worked within. Jillian sucked at the last of the lemon drop, grateful for the small sugar boost, but now her hunger awakened. Again, her dilemma of no money tweaked at her. Soon, however, this wouldn't be problem. Mr. Nahl would let her know where to find Mason and then she'd be on the right track. At last, she was getting somewhere.

The first floor consisted of an attorney's office and another for a gold assayer, while the second had one locked door and a dentist's office. The stairs creaked as she made her way to the third floor where she found a set of empty rooms. She glanced around in dismay. The store owner sent her to the wrong place.

"Hello?" A female voice boomed up the stairway. "If you want to rent the place, stop by the dentist. One floor down."

Jillian hurried down the steps where a sturdy

woman waited. "I understand the artist, Mr. Nahl, has a studio here."

"You're a month too late. Mr. Nahl relocated his studio to San Francisco. He's moved up in the world, so off he goes. No matter. With so many new people in town, the rooms will go fast. Are you interested in renting?"

"I'm a visitor to your city, and will go back home soon," she said. "I did want to speak to Mr. Nahl about a painting he did. The one of the mining town? For Mr. Crocker?"

The woman scratched one armpit. "I don't have much use for art. Didn't see the German fellow too often. He was a quiet sort. Stuck to his own business and always paid his rent on time."

"Did he have many visitors? A man, with an English accent, for instance."

A moan arose from inside the dentist's office followed by a gruff sounding voice. "Flora, come hold him down. The tooth needs to come out."

The woman half-turned from Jillian and rolled up her sleeves. "If you don't intend to rent the place, I can't stand here talking." She shoved open the door to the office. Before it clicked shut behind her, the moans within grew into a howl.

Jillian hurried down the stairs and into the street. She didn't have the money to chase Mr. Nahl to San Francisco. What should she do now?

"There she is!"

Jillian spun in the direction of the familiar voice and froze. Caleb, in the company of Zeb the gardener, pointed straight at her. Just half a block away, they sat atop a small wagon drawn by a sway-backed mare.

Grim-faced, Zeb flicked the reins and the wagon lumbered toward her.

Run, she ordered her feet.

Now.

Chapter Six

Jillian whirled, then strode from the wagon carrying Zeb and Caleb. Behind her, the boy shouted, "Jane, wait!"

Over one shoulder, she glimpsed Zeb pass the reins to the boy and hop off the wagon. She lifted her skirts above her ankles and ran. If she could make it to the next corner...well, she had no idea what might happen next. There appeared nowhere to hide, no safe haven. Steps pounded on the wooden walkway behind her. The chase was on.

A strong hand appeared from nowhere and seized her about the waist, all but yanking her off her feet. Foul breath steamed in her ear. "Why in such a rush, young missy?"

Jillian struggled against the arms that now wrapped her in a vise grip. One hairy hand brushed her breast. She fought to free herself from the man's fondles. As his gropes grew more earnest, she twisted and slammed a knee into the man's crotch. He dropped to his knees and released his grasp; she tumbled to the ground.

"Bitch," he gasped, both hands flying to his injured anatomy.

She scrambled to her feet and backed away from her red-faced attacker, whose huge unkempt gray beard sprouted from his face. His eyes were bleary, and a memory flashed to the courtly homeless man at the train station only a day earlier, in her own time. Then, rules of conduct made sense, and her world seemed trouble-free.

Her hair had tumbled loose from its knot at her neck and fell across her eyes. A pair of women stared at her dishevelment with disapproval evident in their expressions, as though she was the one at fault for creating a ruckus.

The man still strove to grab her. One hand stretched for her while the other cupped his crotch. "Whore. You need a thorough whipping."

Zeb's deep voice rumbled at Jillian's shoulder as he pointed a horsewhip at her assailant. "If anyone needs to be whipped, it's a foul beast like you who assaults a lady on the street."

Caleb ran up, eyes alight with admiration. "Jane, are you all right? You dropped him right to the ground."

The man stumbled to his feet, bent slightly at the waist. "No lady runs, skirts up to display her wares. I just sampled to see if I wanted to buy." He winced as he straightened and edged away. "I see now the hellcat's yours. Good luck to you."

Zeb laid a strong hand on Jillian's shoulder. The gardener towered above her. "The Crockers require you home. There's trouble there." His tone brooked no debate.

She faced the somber-faced man and Caleb. "I-I can explain." She fell silent. They wouldn't believe the truth, and any justification for disobeying March's orders fled her mind.

Business on the street proceeded as usual, with carts and carriages rolling past. The scuffle caused little more than a few cautious glances and a couple of knowing smiles. Her assailant could have dragged her into an alley, and no one might have rescued her. She was trapped in a world where women were either ladies, servants, or whores.

"Amy declares our new maid is a ghost and then you were nowhere to be found." Caleb's explanation rushed forth. "Not a word Mr. and Mrs. Crocker said convinced her otherwise. I've never seen March so hopping mad. You have to show yourself to Amy. You have to prove you ain't a ghost."

Her mouth fell open at Caleb's speech. Twice now the girl had called her a ghost, first to her face and now to others. The Crockers' daughter noticed something peculiar in her, more than her modern attire or that first frightful moment after the earthquake. Neither Zeb nor Caleb mentioned her status as an intruder and interloper. What had the girl perceived that no one else had? Did the child see her materialize out of thin air?

Zeb gestured to the cart where the mare stood placidly. "Let me assist you. Caleb can ride in back."

With trembling fingers, Jillian gathered her loosened hair, and twisted and knotted it at her neck. "Of course," she said, hoping she sounded calm, though her heart raced. "I should speak with the girl at once and ease her mind."

****

The drawing room's double doors stood open. From within, a woman's voice murmured. Jillian approached with trepidation. The next few minutes determined her fate. Mrs. Crocker was sure to question her about her presence in the house. She had no credible story to tender and the truth would deliver her to the madhouse.

"The maid is here," March said, from behind Jillian. The housekeeper had been furious upon her return, but kept the fury confined to a dark glint in her eyes. Jillian had proffered no excuse, but tied on an apron and, with eyes downcast, followed the stiff-backed woman to the drawing room. At the door, March nudged her forward.

"Come in, please." Mrs. Crocker's soft voice matched her appearance with eyes wide and doe-like. Light brown hair threaded with gray wisped loose from pins, and delicate lace fluttered at her throat and wrists. Everything about the woman emanated sympathy and consideration. Her husband stood in front of an unlit fireplace, clad in a black suit, his back ramrod straight. Amy stared wide-eyed, perched next to her mother on a carved wood sofa. The three Crockers examined Jillian, their varied thoughts mirrored in their expressions. The mother relieved, the father impatient, and the daughter stubborn.

Jillian swallowed and entered the room. Her glance darted from Amy to the girl's parents.

"You see, my dear. Flesh and blood." Mrs. Crocker your father and I."

Amy's chin jutted forward, her gaze cool and skeptical. "But she appeared from nowhere, Mama. That's the truth."

Mrs. Crocker tilted her head. "Jane, is it? I must apologize for my daughter's overactive imagination."

"Ma'am, I'm sorry to be the cause of any trouble."

The child glanced up at her parents. "She's like the man I told you about."

Jillian choked back a gasp. "A man?"

Mason.

"There was no man," her mother broke in, patting her daughter's hand while offering Jillian a look of apology. "Amy has a most accelerated imagination for her age."

The girl rose, stomped her foot. "There *was* a man. He lived in another time and wore the strangest attire with the image of a peculiar gray animal on the front of his shirt. He haunted the dining room." She nodded toward Jillian. "Just like her."

Jillian suppressed a shiver. Mason had packed a shirt with a kangaroo on the front for his trip. "This man? Tell us what happened to him?"

Behind her, March cleared her throat softly, a growl, a warning to keep to her place.

"He stood at the window for the longest time," the girl said. "Then asked me what year it was. That's how I knew for certain I met a ghost."

Mr. Crocker, who had silently observed the conversation to this point, rubbed his forehead with one hand. "I believe I've heard enough. Jane is here, and we all see her, plain as day. She is our maid and not a ghost at all. This is a proven fact." Like his wife, he gave Jillian an apologetic smile. "You are a kind young lady, and we are fortunate to have you in our home."

She almost heard March snort fire like a dragon from the doorway. The housekeeper couldn't very well dismiss her now, not with Mr. Crocker's blessing so apparent.

"Thank you," Jillian said.

"You said your head ached, my dear." Mrs. Crocker rose and laid a hand on her husband's shoulder. "Let's get you upstairs, shall we?"

"I've work to do. There will be time for rest later. I will be in my study and wish not to be interrupted." He brushed past his wife and daughter without another word.

Jillian scooted to the side as he passed. His forehead furrowed and skin ashen, he appeared a man seriously ill. She dropped a curtsy to Mrs. Crocker, though perhaps people never curtsied in America. Still, people in the upper classes always liked a bit of subservience.

She returned her focus to Amy. "Where did…"

"Jane." March's voice remained low, yet authoritative. "We're done here. We shall return to the kitchen now."

Jillian didn't budge. The child had witnessed Mason's appearance in this time—it *had* to be him— and perhaps she had a clue as to where he went.

"The man," she started again, and her voice rose, "where did he go?"

Amy gazed solemnly toward her, an adult awareness in her eyes. "Away. He ran, far more frightened of me than I of him." The girl faced her mother. "I displayed no fear. Not one bit."

"My brave girl, let's have a pudding." Mrs. Crocker's lavender skirts rustled as she rose. "I'm sure Mrs. Stevens has a sweet prepared." She glanced toward the housekeeper. "We'll have it in the children's playroom."

"Ma'am," March agreed. "Jane and I will return to the kitchen now and speak with Mrs. Stevens."

As the lowliest of servants who scrubbed dishes and fortunate to sleep in a tiny attic compartment, Jillian had no power in this household. She couldn't compel information from a privileged child of this powerful family. Dismissed, she followed March to the kitchen, aware a tongue-lashing was imminent. As she girded herself, she plotted how to speak to Amy alone.

****

The scolding never came. The housekeeper delivered the request for pudding to the cook and handed Jillian into Mrs. Stevens' care. Then, thin-lipped, she stalked off toward her office.

The cook chuckled as she sliced three servings of bread pudding, studded with raisins. She poured a splash of cream atop each one, set two on a tray and one on the long kitchen worktable. The cook gave her a sidelong glance. "The child raised an almighty commotion earlier when you weren't to be found. Where did she get the notion you were a ghost?"

Jillian studied the pudding and her stomach rumbled in hunger. The aroma of cinnamon and nutmeg drifted up and merged with that of warm bread. "I haven't an idea. Does she see ghosts often?"

"Twice before. This is why the parents were so determined for you be found. They need to curb her wild imagination. You're fortunate that you can't be fired now, though Mrs. March aches to say the words." The cook gestured to the table. "Sit a moment and have a sweet bite, child. Sarah or one of the other maids can take the tray up."

Grateful for the unwarranted kindness, Jillian sank to the chair and nibbled at the moist, cakey pudding. The first sweet mouthful evoked a shadowy memory of a long-ago Christmas. A fireplace crackled, laughter, presents piled in heaps around a huge live fir tree. Had her mother made the bread pudding? Her Aunt Paige?

A grandmother? Tears sprang to her eyes. She'd never felt more alone than in this moment.

I don't belong. Why am I here?

Sarah bustled into the kitchen, out of breath, Mrs. Stevens just behind her. The other maid came to a halt when she spotted Jillian at the table. "I'm to take the puddings up and *she* sits there like the queen of England?"

"Easy, girl, just do as you're told," Mrs. Stevens counseled. "And I doubt you'd find the queen in my kitchen."

"I don't understand why she's so special." Sarah muttered her complaints but took the tray away.

The cook snapped green beans into a bowl at the far end of the table, then whisked the bowl to the side. With scarcely a pause, she sprinkled flour on the wooden surface and plopped down a large round of dough. Mrs. Stevens hummed a soft tune as she rolled out the dough and cut it into biscuit rounds.

Jillian finished her treat and stood, much refreshed. The quiet moment had restored her. "Thank you. I-I don't deserve your kindness after I disobeyed Mrs. March."

The woman shrugged off the compliment. "The world is a difficult place. The Crockers are the finest people I've ever known, and they set an example we all strive to follow."

"What is Mr. Crocker's ailment?"

Mrs. Stevens sighed. "Too much study over the years has tired his brain and made him ill. The doctors fear for his life."

"I don't believe someone can die from too much study. There must be another reason, a medical diagnosis. A minor stroke perhaps?"

"A what? For heaven's sake, what are you going on about?" The cook drew up her shoulders. "A fatigued brain. That *is* the medical diagnosis. The Crockers can afford the best doctors and don't need a new maid's opinion. I should let the household know we mistakenly have a doctor employed as a maid in the house."

"My apologies, Mrs. Stevens," Jillian said quickly. She needed to re-establish herself in the household and make no further missteps.

Jillian carried her dish to the scullery and scrubbed it along with a stack of pots. The constant flow of dishes to clean in a household this size never ended. Whoever invented the automatic dishwasher deserved a medal. And electricity. And pipes that delivered hot water. And modern medical science.

Mrs. Stevens' rosy face peeked around the corner from the kitchen, her good humor restored. "Now, I'm off for my morning rest while the biscuits rise. Can I trust you to behave yourself and not run off again? Someone needs to stay in the kitchen in case the family requires assistance."

She nodded, trying to appear sincere, and her conscience twinged at this constant deception. Escape to the future needled her every waking moment. In the meantime, she needed the protection of this household. The Sacramento of the 1870s was a perilous place for a woman alone.

She displayed her soapy hands. "I'm at your service."

"Good girl." The cook headed off for her nap.

Jillian rinsed and dried the pots and hung them

back in their places in the kitchen. March still hadn't returned, and the other household staff dispersed to other parts of the house. She must take advantage of the moment and do some surveillance. If she acted quick, no one needed to know.

"Sorry, Mrs. Stevens," she murmured, and then proceeded to the kitchen door where stairs led to the family mansion. This house must operate as a portal of some sort. The dining room must contain some sort of a doorway home.

Chapter Seven

A ray of sun cut across the long table and ricocheted off a crystal wineglass. A colorful prism painted the white tablecloth. The ever-present echo of hammering from town filtered through an open window. This elegant room must be admired by many, but Jillian had no time to spare or interest. March or some other member of the household would soon discover her here or find her gone from the scullery; either way meant trouble. So far, she'd been a cat with nine lives, but a life or two might need to be held in reserve until required later.

Jillian returned to the original spot by the window where the earthquake struck and she'd crossed into the past. She studied the floor. Her stomach clenched in fear that a new era might seize her to somewhere further in the past or catapult her to some far future date. This whole situation was crazy, just as a belief that time-travel had rules and likely to drop her off where she started like a roundtrip train ticket. Even if she somehow vanished from this era, Mason would be left behind. She intended to locate the passageway, but not use it—yet.

A low shushing whispered through the window though no breeze swayed the tree branches outside. A tick-tick-tick from a wooden clock on the wall and her rapid breaths were the only other sounds. Jillian ran a hand along the sill, in a search for she-didn't-know-what. A vibration? Nothing called to her, no hint of the strange journey she had taken, which had begun in this room. She circled the dining table, scanned the ceiling, and tapped at the walls. If there was a time portal in this room, it had disappeared. The spirit had been here; he'd waved from this window and appeared the moment of the earthquake.

Are you the key? If so, where are you?

A rattle from behind made her whirl toward the doorway. The young girl, Amy, stood quietly examining her. Around the child's neck wound at least three long strands of pearls, a ruby brooch pinned to the breast of her dress, and numerous rings decorated her fingers. In addition, the child clutched an ornate black lace shawl to her shoulders and topped the ostentatious outfit with an ill-fitting ostrich-feathered hat.

"Hello," the girl said. "I'm Princess Amy. How do you do?" The girl danced into the room in little hops and jumps. She did a twirl, while one hand pinned the hat to her head, and halted before Jillian.

"I'm well, thank you. At least…" Jillian wasn't sure how to deal with this girl. The unusual child had a mystical insight. A glance at the doorway assured her they were alone for the moment. "I had hoped to speak with you again."

"My birthday comes soon," the child said, as she stroked the shawl's delicate lace. "Birthdays are magic times. Mother says I can make a wish at midnight and it will come true." Her large eyes darkened. "I meant to ask for a new pony last year but I fell asleep and my maid didn't wake me as she promised."

The girl believed in magic and ghosts. A child's

fancy or a bit more? Something extraordinary pervaded this house and Amy had witnessed some of it. "What will you ask for this year?"

"To marry a prince, of course."

Jillian nodded to encourage the girl. "A good wish, but one not likely to come true for a few years."

Amy tossed copious chestnut hair about her shoulders. Her eyes glittered with mischief. "I'll have a prince. Maybe two."

The child was much too alert for her years and possessed a wild streak. "Heavens. What would you do with two?"

Amy jutted out a strong jaw. "Not at the same time, silly." Solid heels thudded on the stairs and the girl's head cocked to one side. She backed toward the other arched doorway, on the far side of the room. "Mother doesn't mind if I dress in her jewels. My nanny—my personal maid—doesn't like it, so don't tattle."

Jillian stepped forward as her opportunity started to slip away. "Wait. Tell me. You proclaimed me a ghost when you first saw me. And two others. Do you know where the man is with the gray animal on his shirt? And what do you see about us that is different?"

Amy rose on her tiptoes and twirled in the doorway. "You fade and glow like the others. I'm not afraid, though you don't belong here. The other woman stayed for just a few moments before she vanished. She wore a shiny ball gown, narrow to her ankles, and short hair like a boy. I suppose she didn't like it here." She pointed to the staircase. "The man ran out the door. I watched from the window as he headed toward town."

Goosebumps broke out along Jillian's arms. The girl twirled on her toes and fled the room. Jillian started after her, but a rustle of skirts behind her halted her steps. A heavy-set woman dressed in a white and black narrow-striped dress, jowls heaving, strode into the room from the other side.

"Where is she? I heard her voice. That child is a demon." The woman's eyes widened. "Who are you?"

Jillian desperately wanted to chase after Amy. "A new maid." Was it possible Mason entered the past and his image captured in a famous painting? Not possible; the picture didn't exist until very recently. She almost laughed; none of this was possible. Her mind spun with a blur of fact and fiction.

"The new maid the child's been talking about, I presume." The woman pressed a hand to her bosom as her breaths slowed. "The Crockers are much too indulgent, if you ask me. In my day, parents didn't tolerate ghost stories."

Jillian forced herself to focus on the woman before her. Any person in this house could be helpful with their knowledge of this place and time, if asked the right questions. Her hands gripped the back of a high-backed dining chair and she gave a smile. "I'm sure in your day the ghosts behaved themselves better."

The nanny made the sign of the cross. "If any spirits wander the earth, they deserve their punishment. God takes back his lambs unto his arms."

"The Crocker's youngest daughter is very certain of herself," Jillian ventured. "Perhaps there is more to this world of ours than we understand."

"A willful girl that one." She clucked her tongue. "She needs firm guidance. That's enough understanding for me."

The snap of a whip cracked from the street and

heavy wheels rumbled by. The nearby river's wet, murky scent filtered through the window, carried along by a light breeze.

"You've noted nothing strange about this house, perhaps this very room?"

The woman shrank back and glanced around. "Do you suggest evil spirits lurk?"

Jillian shook her head quickly as she realized her mistake. In her own time, communing with spirits had made her a successful and sought-after woman of business. In the 1870s, not everyone would be as entertained and excited by this unique talent of hers. "I simply wondered where Amy might gather her impressions."

"The mother—" The nanny broke off and pursed her lips. "There are far too many ideas in this house. No wonder the child is confused."

A clatter drew their attention to the doorway where Amy had made her escape. Caleb shifted from foot to foot; his gaze darted from the nanny to Jillian. "Mrs. Stevens requires you in the scullery. There are dishes to wash."

Her shoulders slumped and she gave a wry grin. "Mrs. Stevens must be a magician. She makes dirty dishes appear out of thin air, even when she's at rest." She nodded to the nanny. "I'm Jane, by the way."

"You may call me Miss Temple. And now I should find my charge before she creates trouble somewhere. As she always does."

Caleb gave an impatient gesture. "Come quick, Jane. We're not allowed in the family dining room. March will have our hides."

****

Dishes, pots, and pans to scrub, then silver to re-polish. The staff dinner featured beef stew with yeast rolls, and then more dishes to clean. From the sink, Jillian studied her water-logged fingers, the skin wrinkled and puckered up to her wrists. An ache settled between her shoulders from her hunched position, her feet hurt, and her arm muscles were sore from all the scrubbing. She collapsed onto the cot immediately upon trudging up the stairs to her room, exhausted and more than a little defeated.

What if I can't find Mason? Or return home?

For the first time, the profound truth of her situation struck her. A flutter in her stomach grew and rose to tighten her chest. She clenched her fists. Women throughout history took charge of their own destinies, in much more dire circumstances than her own. True, she had neither money, nor family, nor friends to rely on. Knowledge of the future was only so helpful—after all, telephones, the internet, and central heat were possible, but that didn't mean she knew how to invent them. Most people had no idea how those technologies worked. Space travel, satellites, convection ovens, antibiotics—the long list of modern, *future* inventions would sound like science fiction to people in 1872.

She needed to come up with her strengths and one of those was not being a maid. *I see ghosts. I'm a writer.* Neither helped in this situation. She sat up in bed and swung her feet to the floor. *I know my worth as a person. I may not be able to vote or own property, but I know I'm not second to any person.*

Jillian tugged off her uniform and hung it with care on a hook in a narrow cupboard. On a shelf, someone had placed a corset, plain cotton camisole, and strange underpants—knickers with a peculiar split-open crotch. More clothes to layer into. No wonder the knickers provided a gap; otherwise one could spend a half hour adjusting various garments to relieve oneself.

And speaking of a bathroom, she'd yet to take a bath. After only two days of toil in this warm climate and heavy clothing, her body odor announced her presence, though she wasn't alone in this. Everyone's unique personal scent preceded their arrival into a room. The people in this era bathed less often so her own body odor blended in with everyone else's. Oh, for a lavender scented bar of soap, hibiscus shampoo, or even unscented deodorant.

Anyway, she intended to figure out a way home before the week ended. Fingers crossed.

Out the small window, the dim lights of Sacramento burned. Somewhere in this city Mason breathed and walked and dwelled. She *wasn't* alone, and this bolstered her courage.

Tomorrow, I'll find him.

****

"I require a bolt of gray wool," March said as soon as Jillian reported to the housekeeper's office the next morning. "Sarah is busy changing linens and so I've decided you should return to town for this errand." The woman's throat worked as though she fought back other words. "While you're in town, I wouldn't be averse if you inquired about your intended. We must be charitable toward one another, mustn't we?"

Jillian's eyes widened at the woman's change of heart. "Thank you. I—"

"After all, I was young once, though a very long time ago. Youth is fleeting, especially for the fairer sex.

Some of us have just one prospect for the protection of marriage." The housekeeper stared at a frame on her desk. "Far be it from me to remove your single chance at happiness."

Jillian followed her gaze, to a sepia portrait of a youngish man who clutched a musket, before rising to March's face. A quick calculation told her the man, if indeed the housekeeper's lost love, most likely fought in the Mexican-American war twenty-five years earlier. The Civil War was too recent for the man's and Mrs. March's age and the Spanish-American War still a couple decades away.

"If you find him, you have my best wishes and those of this household," March continued in a soft tone. "Otherwise, return and attend to your duties. The Crockers have taken to you; I owe them too much to allow you to fail here. You could do much worse."

A wave of empathy swept through Jillian, and this impelled her to tell a version of the truth. "Mrs. March, I know he's here and when I find him, we will go home. I'm sorry for the trouble I've caused you, but I don't want you to believe I'll stay. You've been kinder than I deserve."

The housekeeper waved one hand in a dismissive gesture. "Go to town, purchase the wool, and conduct your search. Caleb will accompany you to provide an escort and carry the packages." The woman rose and her tone grew stern. "I hope you find your intended and don't return to service here. I won't pretend you're an asset to my staff. You may go now."

March wanted her gone, one way or another. Jillian didn't take offense or hesitate. She found Caleb waiting for her outside the kitchen door. He appraised her as they strolled the short distance back to town. Gray clouds shrouded the early sun and heavier, darker clouds glided across the sky from the west. From the direction of the Sacramento River drifted a damp, earthy animal smell.

"Mrs. Stevens says Amy has the sight. And Amy believes you're a ghost." He poked her arm. "You seem real enough to me."

"Boo," Jillian said in a matter-of-fact tone, with a glance at the boy. "Did I scare you?"

Caleb chuckled and kicked a stone from their path. They arrived at the edge of the boardwalk and trod on the new wood planks, sawdust at the edges and in the cracks. Two women, bonnets rising high on their heads, long skirts swishing, passed without a glance. Just like in her own day, the lower classes coexisted on a different, invisible plane. A black man shouldered a sack, head and back bent under the burden. A brand the shape of an 's' disfigured one side of his face, the scar puckered at the edges.

Caleb took in her lingering stare at the man, who must have been a former slave. "You know about Mr. Crocker, don't you, and his abolitionist work?"

"I don't know much about him, I'm afraid." History books spoke mainly about his brother, the more famous Crocker as a member of the Big Four railroad partnership which created part of the transcontinental rail system.

Caleb shook his head. "It ran in all the papers. Everyone knows about it here." He filled his lungs with air and blew it out slowly. "He argued all the way to the U.S. Supreme Court to help slaves stay free if they escaped to free states."

She came to a halt. A chill went through her with the realization how far back in history she had traveled, to a time where former slaves lived. "But the war is over. There is no more slavery."

"This happened before the war, before I was born even, but Mr. Crocker is famous for his role with abolition."

Jillian knew this part of history though. "He couldn't have won the decision. The courts ruled on the side of slave owners then. Many runaway slaves were arrested and taken back to a brutal existence."

"He lost the case, but the war showed who was right in the end, didn't it?" Pride infused his tone.

A surge of gratification went through her also, that even though just a maid, she worked in the home of a famous abolitionist.

"Caleb, have there been Chinese workers—or perhaps Chinese friends of the Crockers—in the mansion?"

The boy chuckled in disbelief. "Friends? I'd say not. You're always saying such odd things."

"Right, then how about workers?" She pressed her lips together. Equality hadn't progressed *that* far.

His brow wrinkled. "I don't know what you're going on about. Mr. Crocker doesn't mind the Chinese. He won't have a bad word said about them, even though there's plenty who don't like their ways. Fact is, there's no call for their type of labor at the mansion. Certainly not *inside*."

They continued on. Jillian scanned the faces of those in the street and through windows of stores they passed. Saloons commanded every corner, an apothecary shop, the sheriff's office, a boarding house, a bank. "I suppose a newcomer might not be noticed in a town this big."

The boy threw back his shoulders. He clearly enjoyed his role as expert in various subjects. "I'm in town all the time. Not much gets by me. When did your man travel through here?"

"A day or two ago—" she started and then stopped with the realization she had no idea. The painting changed everything. "Or six months ago, perhaps more."

Caleb frowned and gave her a sidelong glance. "You don't sound too sure of your facts. There *is* a beau, isn't there?"

A man's hearty laugh cut through their conversation and brought her to a standstill. Across the road, in front of a forge, two men chatted next to a set of carriage horses. Both men were rough in appearance, hard-working men with heavy beards, dirt-encrusted denim pants, and well-worn boots. The man on the left—the one with light brown hair—patted one of the horses on its neck, ran his hand expertly down one of the animal's legs, and lifted it to check the shoe. Something about him sent goosebumps prickling down her spine.

Chapter Eight

Jillian's feet moved before her head understood what she was doing.

"Jane," Caleb said. "Where are you going?"

Her gaze riveted on the men, one in particular, she paused to avoid a wagon and mule, and then strode forward. The man, with weathered and deeply-tanned skin, couldn't be Mason but her heart drew her forward. Tears sprang to her eyes. Some anomaly in time dropped her into the 1870s all alone, and desperation overtook her senses. The laugh had been *his*, so close in tone as to be one and the same. Maybe Mason had a double, after all.

He didn't glance her way until she stood at his shoulder. Mason's hazel eyes, his lips under the unfamiliar beard, but broader shoulders, thicker arms, and chapped and scraped hands from arduous physical labor. The similarities and disparities came to her in a glance. They stared at each other for less than a second before his arms wrapped about her, squeezing her tight against his chest.

"Oh God," he breathed into her hair. "Not you, too. Not here. But thank God." He pulled back and stared in disbelief, and then drew her to him again.

"How…?" he started.

"When…?" she asked. This was Mason—but at the same time, *not* Mason. He was so changed.

Caleb ran up. "Jane, is this your beau? Your intended? Not dead from robbers or infected with gold fever?"

The boy's questions buzzed at her ear, but Mason remained her sole focus. "Your beard. Your hands. The painting. This…this place."

Mason regained his senses first and with a glance around them, gripped her shoulders. "We have much to discuss. But not here in the street."

The other man chuckled. "I see you've a secret past, Chandler. I'd best return to my work." He assessed Jillian with a shrewd grin. "The horses need to be shod by first light tomorrow. I'll trust they're in good hands and you'll not be too busy with other, er, activities."

"You know my work," Mason said, the lilt of his Australian accent music to her ears. "Your beauties will be well taken care of." They shook hands, and the other man strode down the boardwalk.

Jillian scooted back to stand next to Caleb and stared, her mouth slightly agape. The man she knew so well had never shod a horse in his life. And now a trusted and known farrier? Only a couple days earlier, she'd seen him in San Francisco. Then, his chin shaved clean, he had no more knowledge of horses than any modern city denizen. Now…not even a week later, his appearance was strikingly different and he'd become a recognized expert in horses. His image captured in a painting by a well-known artist and…she stared. Was that a gray hair? Mesmerized, she stepped closer. More than one silvery strand wove through his beard, and her gaze rested on his whiskers as though they contained the answers she sought.

Mason's familiar hazel eyes studied her in return. A remoteness settled in his expression now as though she were a long-ago acquaintance and nothing more. "Are you in a safe situation?"

"At the Crocker mansion. On the edge of town to the south." She gave a self-deprecating laugh. "I'm a scullery maid."

One of the horses snorted. Mason patted its neck and gripped the bridle. "I'm familiar with the place. My first stop here, you might say."

She glanced at Caleb, who grinned as he witnessed their reunion and would be certain to repeat all he heard and saw of this moment. No matter. She'd found Mason and now everything would be fine. A surge of confidence and happiness swept through her. "I'm certain the house is our key to return."

He gave a brief nod and spoke in a normal tone. "Do you believe your employer might allow you to go for a walk this evening, after your work is done?"

Caleb chuckled. "March is going to split a seam. You never said your man worked as a blacksmith."

Jillian's voice grew low and earnest. She didn't plan to scrub any more dishes. Her time as a maid in 1872 was over. "Don't you think we should stay together now that I've found you? We can go, now, to the house. What if something else occurs to keep us apart?"

Mason gave his head a firm shake. Deep furrows appeared in his forehead. "I've been in Sacramento for three years. Doesn't appear I'm headed anywhere."

She gasped and swallowed a huge lump. This couldn't be possible. "Three years?" The gray hairs threading his beard punctuated the stress and hardships he must have undergone alone. This explained the physical changes and the strange coolness that had descended after his initial reception of her. He must blame her for this situation. "It couldn't be that long."

"Since the big earthquake."

Another glance at Caleb. She mustn't speak of time travel and spirits until she and Mason had privacy. "I felt such an earthquake three days ago."

Mason's eyebrows shot up. "Three days!"

"I don't recall any shaking this week," the boy broke in, and his mouth shifted into a frown. "Nor heard anyone speak about a quake."

Why wouldn't the boy leave them alone to speak freely? She whirled on Caleb with the intent to send him away.

Mason touched her arm and drew her back. "Let's not make waves in our situations, lest the state of affairs gets worse."

"Worse than where we are and who we've become?"

He gestured around them and raised one eyebrow. "We are in this nation's newest capitol city and gainfully employed." He lowered his tone and leaned down so his mouth lay close to her ear. "I've seen men cut down in cold blood, followed by a hanging last week. You've only been here three days versus my three years. Trust me when I tell you there's a harshness we need to respect. When people step out of their roles, there are dire consequences."

His expression darkened into a grimace Jillian had never seen on him. Her own fears of being called out as a liar and intruder swept through her, although that danger had subsided. For now, it appeared, her situation was secure. But what had happened to Mason, trapped in another place and time for three years?

"After the dinner hour, come to the stables." She glanced at Caleb, who nodded his approval. "We can stroll by the river before the house is locked for the night."

****

With the shock of their meeting over, Mason's changed appearance was more familiar. When he arrived at the kitchen's back door that evening, Jillian stepped into his arms and kissed him firmly. As he gripped her around the waist and her body met his, the changes of his past three years grew evident. His shoulders and chest broader and arms more muscular. Once lean, his torso was now more robust and substantial. Whatever challenges Mason had faced, he had fought back and grown stronger.

She drew back and studied his weathered face with stress lines new since the week before, in modern day. "Tell me everything," she demanded. "How did you end up here? In Sacramento and this house? And a farrier. How did that occur? No matter, we must find a way back. I have an idea…the child you met when you first arrived. Her name is Amy. I think she can help…"

He held up a hand to halt the barrage of questions and comments. "One thing at a time. I've had longer here to consider the options. First, I don't believe there's a way back." His mouth tightened and he glanced around then nodded toward the river. "Let's walk. The sound of the water will cover our conversation."

Around them, the night rose with the sound of crickets chirping, a song she always equated with the emergence of stars. As a child, she believed the stars sang; even now, this was a childish notion difficult to give up. Mason strode a half step in front of her so she had to nearly jog to keep up. At the river's edge he slowed, his chin lowered almost to his chest. He stared over the slow-moving current.

"There's so much to tell you, I don't know where to begin."

A lump filled her throat. "How did you end up here? I last saw you in San Francisco."

His jaw tightened. "I lied to you about my trip. I intended to surprise you on the train, the one you ticketed." He shook his head, as though in wonder. "That seems a lifetime ago. I stayed in the city, met with a couple of friends, and then drove to Sacramento. Like you, I had a free day before our evening train. I saw a poster for a photography exhibit in the museum."

"You went to the museum," she burst in, "just as I did. What a strange coincidence. We could have run into each other there. I must have just missed you." Her eyes widened in wonder. There must be a reason why they both experienced this uncanny occurrence, some otherworldly power that drew them to the museum. She grasped at his hand with both of hers. "I tried to call you, but someone else answered..." Her voice trailed off as she realized why Mason hadn't answered his cell phone. "You were already gone, weren't you?"

He shrugged and withdrew his hand. They halted and she searched his face. A distance divided them, and she had to remind herself it had been three years for him. Did he blame her for his tumble through time and the resulting struggles he suffered? If it wasn't for her, after all, he wouldn't have traveled to Sacramento.

"As soon as I set foot in the original house, an earthquake struck," he said. "A dizziness overtook me. For a moment I perceived only blackness. Then…" He gestured around them, the meaning clear that he meant 1872. "There was a little girl, and furniture that hadn't been there a moment earlier."

"Amy! She's the Crockers' youngest daughter; she saw you and…" The puzzle of the picture struck her. "Your exact likeness is in a painting that hangs in the mansion."

He held up a hand to stop her words. "The picture came later. So, it's in the museum, I mean house, now." He chuckled without mirth. "Not a museum yet, not for more than a hundred years from now."

A bitterness infused his tone, a characteristic she'd never heard in him before. His mellow nature had hardened under the arduous life he'd endured.

"There I was, heading down a dirt street, the place transformed. Horses and wagons. Old-fashioned clothes. People stared at me dressed in khakis and a polo shirt, wearing aftershave, with little but a wallet full of useless money and credit cards in my pocket. I had my phone and tried to call you. I tried to call my friend, Garth, in San Francisco, my editor, my family in Melbourne. My phone didn't work, you understand, but I tried and tried. I was sure I had gone crazy, or inadvertently swallowed some type of drug, or in a nightmare."

They stared at the river. Her own experience was so much easier, softened by the immediate assumption from March that she had been hired as a maid. From the first hour, she had shelter, clothes, and food provided as she acclimated to this strange situation. Mason had none of those advantages.

He rubbed one hand over his whiskers and continued. "Men don't have tolerance for strangers dressed in a peculiar manner and with a strange accent. I wandered the city for an hour before three men jumped me. They took almost all I had from my pockets, and when they observed my unfamiliar belongings, they beat me again. Try explaining car keys to people in this century. I lost a tooth in that battle." To Jillian's horror, he opened his mouth and pointed to a gap halfway back. "I'm pretty sure they cracked a couple of ribs. I ached for months."

"Mason," she gasped. "That's terrible."

"The first three months were the worst. I must have lost thirty pounds. But reality seeped in and I did what a lot of men do here in these times when they have no other skills. I sold myself as a laborer in the goldfields. I worked digging claims for others in trade for food and shelter. That's where I first learned to tend to horses and found I have a flair for it." He grinned, and in the dim light flickered the old Mason she knew and loved. "I became good friends with the man who owned half the claim, and he introduced me to a painter who traveled to our camp."

"Mr. Nahl."

"Yes, Charles Nahl. I speak a bit of German so we got along fine. He drew some sketches of me; said a Sacramento businessman commissioned a painting." He gave a low whistle. "It ended up in the Crocker house, where you work? The universe is playing cruel games with us."

"Not cruel at all," she said. "If I hadn't seen the picture, I might never have known you were here.

There's a mystery at work here, but I can't figure out what it is."

Purple and red lit the western sky as the sun disappeared below the horizon. A flock of ducks numbering in the hundreds rose out of the fields on the opposite riverbank. With a cacophony of quacks, they circled over the water and flew away. Not until they disappeared did Mason speak again.

"I spent sixteen months in the camp and then Ernest, my friend, tired of the rough life. He invited me to return home with him, to Sacramento, where he said his father could offer me a good job. His father owns several hotels here, along with the blacksmith's where you found me today. Turns out, I'm a natural with horses and with the forge."

Jillian calculated that must have been just over a year earlier. "I can't believe what you've been through, all you've done." She laid a hand on his arm. "Mason, I'm so proud of you. Now we have to figure out how to get back, together. We know time travel exists, so we should be able to reverse this process."

His hazel eyes narrowed somewhat, and his gaze traveled over her. "Jillian, I've been here three years. Three years! Do you understand how long that is when you've struggled to survive, and then to create a new life from scratch? Everything starts over."

She cocked her head to one side and took a step back. "What do you mean? That you don't want to go home? That you've made *this* your home?" She gestured around toward the half-built city, flat farmlands, the river, and a stand of oaks. "I'm not talking about the luxuries of modern day, but no antibiotics or homes with insulation. Most people from these times are dead by the time they're sixty. Two world wars ahead. Our grandchildren." Her face heated because they'd never discussed a future together, but she forged ahead. "Our sons or grandsons might die in those wars. During the three days I've been here, I've had time to consider what a curse it would be to foretell the future, every historic tragedy that looms, and not a thing I could do about it."

He nodded and his throat worked. "I've also considered this and the small role I might play for people close to me, the few lives I might be able to save. I owe a huge debt of gratitude to Ernest and his family, Jillian. Without them, I'd be lost in a world where I didn't belong. If I knew you'd end up here too, I'd have waited, done things in a different manner." He groaned and shifted away from her. He swiped a hand across his eyes, and in profile she saw they glistened with tears.

She gripped his arm, frightened. What did he mean; had he killed a man, or performed a deed so terrible that bound him to these people? He needed reassurance. In the past, they'd relied on each other and gotten through obstacles which had bonded them together. "Whatever you've done to survive, I understand. We can brainstorm together and write a list of places your friends need to avoid on certain dates. Actions they should and shouldn't take. You can leave it for them and over time, they'll see the truth you've written, and they'll know to trust it."

After taking a breath, she forced a laugh, the sound ringing desperate even in her own ears. "We can tell them where to buy land, which stocks to buy and when to sell. You'd make them and their ancestors rich."

The colors in the sky faded as dusk set in, and shadows grew heavy near trees and bushes.

"There's one more thing I must tell you." He gazed at the river, where the rising moon's reflection rippled across the dark water. Dread swelled in her. "This will come hard, I know. There's just no way to prepare you for what I'm about to say. Jillian, I'm engaged to be married."

Chapter Nine

Almost unable to believe Mason, these words more than any other, struck her to the core. As a distraught sound burst from her throat, her knees buckled. He held her elbow and led her to a fallen tree.

"Sit while I explain." Regret laced his voice. He paced in front of her.

"No, don't give details." Only days ago, they had loved each other late into the night, and fallen asleep wrapped in each other's arms. A future together always assumed, or so she'd thought. Today, he was engaged to someone else. Anger at the injustice of their pell-mell tumble through time, each thrust along a separate route, prompted her to lash out. "Yes, as a matter of fact, tell me how you replaced me so fast."

He stopped before her. "Not fast. Three years, Jillian, and stuck in another era, another bloody century. I didn't replace you; we were all but dead to each other."

She rose and faced him. Blood surged to her face. "Who is she, this woman you plan to marry?"

"Ernest's sister. I—"

She cut him off, wanting to wound him for her own pain, even though this wasn't fair. Hiking up the skirts of this ridiculous too-long dress that constrained any woman's stride, she marched toward the house. "Don't tell me you're to marry the boss' daughter."

He strode after her, a half pace behind her. "Jillian, it's not like that at all. You know better than to accuse me of such shallowness."

"Go away, Mason," she called over her shoulder, vision blurred with anger and hurt. "The mansion doors will be locked shortly, and I can't lose my position."

Leaves crunched as he followed. His footfalls fell farther in her wake. "I have more to tell you. We can't part like this."

Her face hot and chest thumping, she swung open the kitchen door. "Goodbye, Mason."

Inside, the door slammed shut, she leaned back against it and let the tears come. The universe had played a cruel trick on them. It cast them apart and then reunited them for no reason but to foment anguish.

March's stern voice interrupted her sobs. "Jane, whatever is the matter? Why the commotion and tears?"

Jillian straightened and hurried across the kitchen toward the servants' stairway. All she wanted to do was throw herself in bed and cry, alone and in private like an injured animal.

"Stop, girl, this instant." The housekeeper's tone came sharp and Jillian reluctantly halted. "This household is responsible for you. If your honor has been insulted, best say so now."

Jillian swiped at her tears and swallowed. "Mrs. March, I'd like to go to my room. This is a personal affair."

The woman shook her head, her mien grim. "What happens to staff is my business. A young woman should not be out after dark with a man. I allowed it because you are betrothed. Caleb tells me you found your man, hale and hearty, employed at the forge. I wonder how it is that he never sent you a letter, and you had to travel here without a protector to find him. I fear he has not been true."

Her unbelievable story threatened to spill out. She bit her lip until the taste of blood flooded her mouth. "Time…time…divided us."

"And you are no longer betrothed?"

"No." Of course, there never had been an engagement. But her heart wasn't any less broken. She parted with Mason for a business trip. Days later she discovered him set to marry another woman.

"A man who runs away from responsibilities deserves punishment," Mrs. March proclaimed. "I'm sure Mr. Crocker can suggest an attorney who will file a breach of contract suit on your behalf. This scoundrel will either marry you or pay for your suffering. I will speak to Mrs. Crocker in the morning."

Dismayed, she blurted, "No, ma'am, please don't."

"This is my duty and the obligation of good-minded people. If your former suitor is not called to task, he may prey on other honest women. A civilized society needs rules as well as those who uphold them. Leave it to me, dear." The housekeeper swept out of the room, head held high.

"Oh, for crissakes," Jillian groaned, and glared at the ceiling. "What's next?"

****

The last thing she wanted was to haul Mason to court. First, because she lied about an engagement. Second, because their true story could never be told; they'd be laughed out of court. Third, and most of all, because she loved him.

She lay on the thin cot in her bedroom, hands

balled into fists. Their separation mere days ago for her, but three years for him. If the situation were reversed, might she move on with her life too? Her heart ached, but she hadn't stopped to consider his feelings. In the first days and months, he must have suffered the pain of their separation along with the loss of everything familiar. Three years from now, her pain ought to ease as well.

The hardest part was never experiencing any coolness to their relationship, no lull in passion nor had boredom set in. All the usual reasons why love affairs ended didn't count here. One day they were inseparable, and on the next the world played a dirty trick on them.

Tomorrow, she would waylay March and confess her lie about an engagement. If the well-known Crockers became involved, Mason's job and position in the community could be damaged. He might lose his fiancée. If he truly preferred to stay in 1872, then let him be happy. Better for her to acknowledge this lie than for a breach of contract suit to proceed.

Tears pooled at the corners of her eyes. Once assured Mason wouldn't suffer from her falsehood, she would tear the dining room apart to find the time portal and get the hell out of this century.

She blinked the tears away as a new possibility occurred to her. What happened when she returned, to a time when Mason never existed? Might her love evaporate or would memories stay? If Mason lived two lives, more than a century apart, was there the possibility of meeting one of his descendants?

A dizzying number of questions flitted through her mind. Time travel made no sense to linear creatures.

People drew breath, lived, then died. In that order. They didn't get to live and die *before* they existed. Of course, all the usual suppositions persisted about whether someone had the ability to change the course of history, and perhaps impact whether they ever drew breath at all. Could she wink out of existence if she changed the past?

The night dragged as her mind raced around, like a rat trapped in a cage. Footsteps sounded below and doors elsewhere in the house opened and closed. Finally, silence set in, but sleep evaded her. When the first pink rays of dawn lit the sky, still she stared at the ceiling. With a heavy sigh, she rose with the intent to find March. Best get her confession over with as soon as possible.

The aroma of coffee, biscuits, and bacon greeted her on the servants' stairs as she descended to the kitchen. The heavy iron stove radiated heat and every window in the kitchen open to let in cooler morning air. Mrs. Stevens stirred a pot, the contents of which appeared to be a thin broth. The two stable boys, along with Emily and Zeb, sat at the table eating their breakfast.

"Good morning, Jane," the cook welcomed her. "Have yourself a good breakfast, you'll be busy today. Sarah has gone to care for a sick sister and Mrs. March won't be down until later. You'll need to pick up the slack."

"I must speak to Mrs. March, about an important matter, as soon as possible."

"Mr. Crocker took ill in the night. Mrs. March sat up with him so the missus could get some rest. What has you worried?"

"I'd rather not say. It's a private affair." Surely, the housekeeper wouldn't mention a maid's personal issues with the Crockers in the midst of a family illness. Jillian twisted her hands together.

The young maid, Emily, giggled and covered her mouth. "Have you set your wedding date?"

Heat rose in Jillian's face. The household help, of course, didn't know of her disastrous clash with Mason the evening before. "No." She poured a cup of the heavy, black coffee and scraped back a chair. The dark liquid steamed and released a strong scent of roasted beans. The first sip burned her lips and she welcomed the distraction of the pain.

"Pass the gal some food," Zeb ordered one of the stable boys.

Emily's eyes widened. "Caleb says your man is a blacksmith. He must be awfully strong. I wonder if I've seen him in town. Is he very handsome?" She giggled again.

"Let Jane have her breakfast," Mrs. Stevens broke in. "You girls need to change linens, dust, and sweep. Dishes first, Jane, then Emily can show you what to do. Mrs. March expects all tasks done as usual."

Grateful for a reason not to talk, Jillian dug into the eggs and biscuits between sips of coffee. One stumbling block had recurred to her in the dark of the night. There must be a reason why she and Mason ended up in this time and place. If she couldn't discover the purpose, she might be trapped here. Was her ability to see spirits the reason she traveled back in time?

Mouth full, she glanced at each face at the table. Not the boys, not the young maid. If she focused and sometimes even if she didn't, a sixth sense for unsettled life-forces surfaced. Zeb? Mrs. Stevens? These older folks surely suffered losses during their lives. The image of a child hovered around Zeb, but the young soul appeared satisfied with its existence. Not Mrs. Stevens either. In the broad scheme of things, few spirits remained in this world, otherwise Earth would teem with ghosts. Who then might need her help? Had it been Amy all along, the sensitive little girl—or the mother, who the nanny inferred practiced a spiritual life?

The stable boys left the table, soon followed by Zeb. Emily hovered, her gaze alternated between Mrs. Stevens and Jillian. "I could help wash dishes, and then Jane and I could do the other chores together," she offered, eyebrows raised.

The cook snorted. "And gossip like a goose, I expect. Get on, girl, with your dusting before Mrs. Crocker and the girls rise. Jane can carry breakfast trays to the family when they summon. I doubt any of them will breakfast in the dining room after the night's hubbub. Mr. Crocker's brain is bleeding again, I expect. The doctor called in again last night. I always said too much study affects the brain. Books give me a terrible headache."

Jillian bit her lip though she wanted to give the cook a lesson in medical science. A brain bleed meant a stroke, an event often referred to as apoplexy in the nineteenth century. The young maid scurried away and Jillian carried the staff's dishes to the scullery. She scrubbed them quickly with hot water toted from the stove top, her hopes raised by the order to serve breakfast to the Crockers. Might she have an opportunity for a quick word with March to stave off a lawyer's involvement? This time, when she saw Amy, she would pay more attention to the girl's aura and less to her words.

On her second trip to fetch hot water, trays were lined up on the table. The cook bustled from table to stove and back again, loading trays with china dishes laden with breakfast fare. "Hurry, the bell for the girls has rung and Mrs. March too. The scullery can wait. Take this broth and coffee to Mr. Crocker's room right away. Don't delay but return for the girls' tray."

Saved by the bells, she thought. Carrying the heavy tray, she climbed the staff stairs to the upper floor where the family had their bedrooms. A main staircase split the broad hallway, with the master bedroom at one end and the children's rooms at the other. Two other bedrooms, used for visitors, were in the middle as well as a playroom. She tapped on the large double doors of the master bedroom. A rustle within, and soft steps approached. The door opened and Mrs. March's face appeared.

The housekeeper swung the door wider and pointed to a table. "Set the tray there," she said in a soft voice.

Jillian glanced at the huge carved wood bed as she tiptoed across the room. Mr. Crocker's eyes lay closed on his sallow face, his breaths deep and even. His long gray beard lay atop the heavy silk covers. Matching silk drapery shrouded the windows, all but a dim filtered light blocked from the room. She set down the tray without a sound. It occurred to her that, if all went well, she might be home that very afternoon, even within the hour. Just one thing needed to be accomplished before her return, if indeed she *could* return.

She drew near the other woman, who hovered at

the doorway, and lowered her voice to a whisper. "Mrs. March, about what you said yesterday. I don't want to sue for breach of contract."

The housekeeper gave her a dark look. "Heavens, girl," she hissed. "Your personal matters can wait. Don't you see this man is very ill?"

Jillian hesitated, knowing full well her appeal came at a grossly inappropriate place and moment. Each hour she waited, however, meant another hour spent in the nineteenth century. And who could say how long Mr. Crocker would lay abed and require round-the-clock care? Days, or even weeks? "A simple request. Just say you won't pursue this, and I'll never mention it again."

Mrs. March seized her by the upper arm and thrust her through the doorway. "Selfish girl. Out."

The door clicked shut and Jillian found herself alone in the hallway. The housekeeper was right to be repelled by her request, but this nightmare must end. All she could do was hope Mason suffered no harm once she disappeared. Her stomach twisted at the thought of leaving him behind.

On the return journey to the kitchen, Jillian took a circuitous route. She needed to see the painting again and so padded down the long corridor to the gallery building. Mason with pen to paper on the right side and, again, with fists raised on the left side. Good and evil. Would this be her last memory of him? "Goodbye, Mason," she murmured, and then twisted away. He created a new life without her, and she must do the same. But hers needed to be somewhere in the future. She'd never survive in this place, with the knowledge he wed another woman.

With renewed determination, she marched to the

dining room and glared around the space. Again, at the window, she tapped the pane and around the sill. What had she been doing when the earthquake hit? Her phone had been in one hand, but the device clattered to the floor when she fell and tumbled into a different century. There would be no way to recreate the original scene, since every detail was changed—no guard watching her, the furniture different, her attire altered. That spirit, who never appeared to her again, and must have been from a different time period altogether. She laid her cheek against the wall and closed her eyes.

Please, let me go home.

A low vibration hummed against her face as though the house responded to her plea. Her heart beat faster and she laid both hands against the wall.

Thank God. This nightmare is coming to an end.

Chapter Ten

Jillian didn't want to open her eyes, fearful beyond her lids lay a street with horses and carriages, and not SUVs and skyscrapers. The thrumming against her face and hands remained, and this heartened her that the universe at last worked in her favor.

Guilt swept through her at the decision to give up on Mason and leave him in a bygone century. She had found him, though. He'd made his choice, with a safe and happy future before him. Her heartache would ease over time, just as his had, and life would once more take on a semblance of normality.

How long did this return journey take—two minutes? Five? Would the guard's sharp voice come to reprimand her for touching the paneling? A man-shaped shadow flickered under her eyelids. She peeked open one eye and then the other. No one was near her who could have created the shadow. At the doorway, Emily stood, mouth agape, hands clutched to her chest. "Jane, are you ill?"

Despair flooded Jillian's body and her shoulders slumped. Still here, unmoved in time. With a hand against the wall, the vibration dissipated—and now gone altogether—she shook her head. "I just needed a moment to myself."

The young maid glanced around the room, her mouth downturned. "Mrs. Stevens said to search for you in here, that you haunt the family dining room. What a thing to say, with our employer nearly dead upstairs."

Jillian head snapped up at the word haunt. The walls no longer trembled and her opportunity lost. She'd confirmed, however, that the room contained a preternatural energy and provided a passageway home, if she figured out how to harness it.

Who was the shadowy essence that had appeared in this room? What spirit dogged her steps, but refused to speak to her?

"Jane!" Emily's anxious tone interrupted her rumination. The young maid glanced over her shoulder and twisted her hands together. "I'm to fetch you downstairs. Your man is here to see you, at the kitchen door."

Mason! Hope and heartache surged through her in equal measure. She'd said her goodbye to him—in person and in her heart. There was nothing he might say, no further explanation to salve her pain. For a half-second, she considered to refuse to see him, but just as quickly reconsidered.

She hurried behind the other maid down the staff stairs, into the warm kitchen where Mrs. Stevens rolled yeasty-scented dough on the floured table. The cook waggled her chin toward the door. "Your beau is most anxious. Out in the yard. Five minutes and then back inside with you. Chores don't get finished by magic."

Jillian opened the door, while Mrs. Stevens' continued to grumble. Several yards away, Mason faced her; his familiar auburn hair and hazel eyes, a new powerful build, all enticed her. At once, her resolve to leave him crumbled. A rush of thoughts tumbled through her mind. She would stay and be his mistress if he desired. If he didn't, she would woo him back. She'd be a homewrecker, a wanton woman, an adulteress, anything that might enable her to be with him again. Those notions battled the reality of Mason's stern demeanor and stiff posture. He didn't want her anymore.

She closed the door and joined him in the yard, coming to a halt several feet away. "I have to go back inside in a couple of minutes." She swallowed back a mountain full of loving, pleading words. "Why did you come back?"

His gaze traveled over her, as though he memorized every detail. "You didn't let me explain the circumstances of my engagement."

Jillian gripped her apron, keenly aware she wore no makeup and wore unattractive clothes. The boss' daughter would be beautiful and dressed in the finery of the times. She had never known jealousy like this before, this awful sickening, stomach-twisting feeling. "The reasons don't matter, do they?"

He gave a snort of frustration and his voice rose. "I think they do." He took a step toward her. "Evaline—my fiancée—is pregnant. Not mine," he added quickly. "But her father doesn't know. He can't know or she'll be ruined. She'd be disowned." His lips twitched as though he prepared to add something more.

A frisson of sympathy coursed through her for a woman giving birth out of wedlock in these times. "You want to save her."

"I gave up on ever getting home again, but I never gave up on my love for you, Jillian. This is what I wanted you to know. Ernest begged me to help his sister. I owe Ernest and his family so much. This is one means I can take to pay them back. Even if a way to return with you existed, I could never forgive myself if I abandoned Eva after pledging a promise." His voice grew hoarse. "You should see her face when she talks about this child and the man she loved."

The affection between Mason and Evaline was obvious, or he wouldn't be so torn. But the story touched her heart and, God help her, made her love him more. "I'm glad you made this effort to tell me. Thank you." She laid a hand on his. "I was shocked and hurt last night, but you didn't deserve my anger. As you said, you've been here three years. I know you've done nothing wrong."

He gripped her hand between both of his, and rough calluses scraped against her palm and knuckles. "I never imagined things turning out this way."

"No, nor I." His hands remained on her and her heart twisted in pain. The idea she had earlier returned to her mind, that if she stayed, they might still somehow be together. "Mason," she started. She meant to tell him, but then she fell silent. Wouldn't it be better if she left him to start a life with Eva? Life here meant committing to a maid's drudgery, being second in his life, and living in a bygone century?

He raised his eyebrows.

"When is the wedding?" she asked instead and swallowed her cowardice.

"Saturday."

"Oh." Her knees trembled. This was Wednesday. Her voice went small. "So soon."

"It'll be a small affair. The child will be born early, less than nine months after our wedding, of course.

There will be more challenges ahead for her. But I've sworn to stand by her side."

"Childbirth is dangerous in these times," she agreed. Again, she suspected he held back more. But she had no right to demand his secrets. Still he clasped her hand, and the electric heat there had always been between them crackled. "You must love her very much."

"I…am grateful, and beholden. You know me well enough, Jillian, to realize I don't break my promises."

He didn't acknowledge he loved Eva, and her pain lifted a touch. An idea came to her. "There is another way. Stay married until the child comes." Her heart beat faster at the terrible suggestion she was about to make. What if he rejected this as well? She finished in a rush. "Then, leave her and return to our time with me. She would still be able to keep her child. Her family is wealthy. They would take care of her."

The kitchen door opened behind her. Mrs. Stevens' voice rang out. "Jane. Enough now. Send your young man on his way."

She didn't take her gaze off Mason's face. "One more minute, Mrs. Stevens. Let me say goodbye."

"Doesn't take so long to say a short word," the cook grumbled, but the door clicked shut.

"I couldn't abandon Eva in that manner, without an explanation. She'd be humiliated and there are other complications…" Mason broke off and frowned at her. There was consideration in his tone. "I'd have to tell her I never will return and provide a reason. Otherwise, she might wait forever for my return." His eyes blazed. "You're certain there's a way out of here?"

"I believe so. There's an energy in the dining room.

I felt it just a little while ago." Jillian glanced over her shoulder. "I'll need to go before our cook busts a gut. Mr. Crocker had another stroke in the night, one of the maids is out, and the household is in upheaval today."

Mason flipped her hand over and examined her palm as though he read their future there. Then he raised it to his lips and drew her close. "I'm afraid to hope, both for a return and to be with you again. But...if there's a chance...maybe there's a way." His voice trailed off. Lines furrowed his forehead.

Her stomach fluttered, even as guilt prickled at her conscience. Her success meant another's loss. Women remarried, and surely Eva could regain her lofty position in society after Mason left.

"Maybe I ended up here to rescue you. Return this evening and we can plan."

****

The rest of the day passed by as fast as a day in drudgery possibly could. At least the household utilized a Chinese laundry service, so she was spared this one chore. How demeaning to wash her co-workers' underclothes, along with those of her employers'. Thomas Edison and his electric lights, still ten years away, would ultimately spur a flurry of labor-saving innovations that untethered women from the home. For now, however, no dishwashers in homes meant she had a secure job as a scullery maid. But perhaps not for long. As much as she suffered overnight, now her heart soared in hope. Mason never forgot her and still loved her! And he halfway agreed to the suggestion to leave Eva.

She'd have to resign herself to the need for Mason to marry this other woman and even honeymoon with her. Her very soul rebelled against this idea, but otherwise Eva faced ostracism. Few men would do what Mason prepared to do for this woman. And few women would put up with her lover set to marry another. The protection of a mother and child, though— wasn't that reason enough? She must throw herself into this heart-rending mission, just as Mason had, and leave the nineteenth century a little better than when she arrived.

Finally, the sun angled low in the sky and chores were completed. More fatigued than ever, Jillian devoured a savory dinner of chicken pot pie and hearty dumplings with an appetite stimulated by physical labor. Mrs. Stevens assigned Caleb to the scullery after the meal so she might meet with Mason. Jillian had to admit that if one had to be a maid, the kindness of the people within this household couldn't be surpassed.

"Jillian," Mason murmured as he enfolded her in his arms. "God, it's been so long."

Without a word, she lifted her face and an equal desire flared in his expression. His lips were warm and firm on hers, and his hands lowered from her waist to search her skirts for her slender curves.

She broke away with a gasp. "We're going to be a scandal if we continue like this."

He grasped her hand, and they hurried toward the river and the shadows of tall oaks and brush. "Here, quick now," he said, and backed her against a tree.

Bullfrogs croaked, crickets chimed in, and the night sounds covered her gasps. A cool breeze wafted off the water and the scent of grass filled her senses. She felt no shame in this impetuous joining. They belonged to each other. If there had been other women in his past three years, they were unimportant because he supposed himself caught in a slip of time. Through it all, Mason never forgot her. Again, she marveled at the changes in his body during his episode here. Not an inch of softness anywhere, not that he'd ever run to flab. This, however, was heavy muscle built not from a gym, but from rigorous outdoor toil.

Breathless and sated, they grew still against each other.

"Wow. Time-travel sex." She flashed a grin at him and arranged her skirts. "Maybe worth the journey."

His low chuckle, unchanged, vibrated deliciously against her chest. "As long as we get back our old lives."

"Then you are agreed, to return."

In answer, he drew her against his body and heat rose in her once more. No one had ever elicited this constant hunger in her before. His warm mouth covered hers and tempted her to hike her skirts again, lost in feverish yearning. The realization they had limited time to plan made her break away.

"Do you think Eva could believe the truth of our situation?"

His lips thinned. "I scarcely believe it myself, even after three years. I've accepted it, but in the way one accepts a dream while asleep."

The river lapped at its banks, a couple feet higher than the day before. No dams impeded snow melt from the lofty Sierra Nevada to the east, and the water rushed downward toward the sea. With a start, Jillian recalled Sacramento's history of frequent floods in the days before high levees contained the two rivers which flowed through its center.

Foreknowledge of history. That was their superpower. "You might convince her if you gave a list of future events."

They brainstormed their knowledge of California history to compile a list, close enough in the future, to prove his story.

"I know as much about California history as you do about Melbourne's," he said with a wry smile. "The Gold Rush and Hollywood about sums it up for me."

"Women won the vote in California about a decade before the national amendment, but I can't recall the exact date," Jillian said. "The San Francisco earthquake though is 1906. Warn her to stay clear."

He shook his head. "That's thirty years in the future. We need events that are more immediate."

The silent, dark water swallowed the last rays of daylight, and a cacophony of crows emanated from huge oaks scattered on the far bank. Swirls of gnats rose from the grass, and a small animal or bird rustled nearby. The pounding of hammers from town had stilled, and the peaceful evening contrasted with her turbulent thoughts.

"There was a governor about this time, with the last name of Booth, a cousin of John Wilkes Booth who killed President Lincoln. Let's see, after the current president, Ulysses S. Grant, comes Rutherford B. Hayes, then Chester Arthur."

Mason nodded. "Those are good. What else?"

Her eyes lit up as she recalled long-ago history lessons. "The telephone! It was invented in 1876, just a few years away. This is a technology no one could guess. The foreknowledge would prove you've told her the truth."

"Of course. National history, world history—as long as the event is significant enough, Eva can confirm these events through the newspapers."

"The Statue of Liberty and the Eiffel Tower, though those don't occur for another decade." Her voice grew more animated the more she recalled. "But how can you not tell her about the wonders to come. The radio and movies. Cars and airplanes. Hot water and indoor plumbing in all houses, not just for the rich."

He snapped his fingers. "There are no modern cameras and film. Those are on the near horizon." He sagged against the tree trunk. "I haven't taken a photograph in three years."

"You will, soon," she reassured him.

"Not only good events are ahead, Jillian. The 1889 flu pandemic, and the Spanish Flu thirty years later—these are events in her lifetime that will kill millions. And what about the wars to come that will slaughter millions more?"

"Not too many negative occurrences, and remember nothing too far in the future either," she said, as her mood grew somber. "Otherwise, you'll leave her with anxiety and fear for what's ahead. She'll need hope for her child and coming generations."

He straightened and set his hands on her waist. "We owe Eva the whole truth. There's no way to tell just part of the story."

"*We?*"

"She needs to know about you," he said. "Tomorrow, I want you to meet her."

Chapter Eleven

Jillian and Mason met his fiancée at the back of the forge where the horses were stabled, and a private conversation might take place. Evaline McAlister appeared barely twenty and had a heart-shaped face and full rosy lips. Ebony hair fell in a heavy tumble of waves down her back and was tied back with a pink ribbon. Dove gray gloves adorned her hands and wrists.

Dark jealousy rose in Jillian. Mason couldn't be immune to Eva's beauty. She'd have to be crazy to send him to the altar with this lovely woman. What if, once wed, he changed his mind and decided to remain with this delicate nineteenth century woman?

"I see why he loves you," Eva said, as her gaze raked over Jillian from head to toe. "You are very pretty. Your hair is the color of spun gold."

The words, so generously given, loosened Jillian's edginess. Mason had already told his fiancée the worst of it, that he loved someone else. Here they stood, to convince her of the rest of it. Nerves at meeting his fiancée was compounded by the fact she'd crept out of the Crocker house that morning, ignoring the renewed heap of pots and pans waiting to be scrubbed. There would be hell to pay when she returned.

"Mason tells me you consent to our marriage for the sake of my reputation," the woman continued, a tremble entering her voice. "God bless you. I can't thank you enough."

Doubts continued to niggle at Jillian. Men would line up to marry a young woman so beautiful and give her child a name. Why did the man have to be Mason? "Can I ask, what happened to the father?"

"I suspect he left Sacramento in case my father learned of our liaison and chose to kill him." Though she spoke directly to Jillian, Eva's wide green-eyed gaze remained on Mason. "My child may favor his father in appearance. Once he is born, there's no way to conceal who he belonged to."

"I don't understand."

Mason laid an encouraging hand on Eva's arm, an intimate gesture that sparked another surge of possessiveness in Jillian. "Eva, you can trust her with your life. Then we will share our own secrets."

"Lin is Chinese." Eva's eyes flashed in defiance. "His family owns a tailor shop and they made clothing for my father's workers. I don't know where he is now, but I hope he remains hidden until we can be together. We must be careful no one suspects our relationship. If my father doesn't kill him first, he may have Lin arrested and sent back to China."

Jillian knew this was just one part of the ugly history from the late nineteenth century. The hatred of Chinese grew steadily after a flood of workers voyaged across the ocean to work in the goldmines and on the railroads. Within the next decade, laws would be enacted to exclude Chinese from immigrating. Already, the law forbade people to marry someone of another race. Should she mention the discrimination promised to grow worse? It was clear now why Eva would have difficulty finding a husband willing to accept a child of half-Chinese ancestry.

"How will your marriage change this situation?" she said. "If it becomes evident the child is one-half Chinese, your father will still be furious."

"Lin will come back for me when he can. My condition will be noticeable soon and a wedding will protect me until the baby is born. After that…" Raising a hand to her mouth, Eva lowered her chin and gave a small sob.

Mason shifted toward her in a protective manner. "We may need to leave Sacramento for the birth. One idea is for Eva to have the child in San Francisco and we'll return with a story of how she lost the child and we adopted another to ease our pain."

At the edge of Jillian's vision, a shadow flickered briefly, like the flick of a hummingbird's wing. She passed it off as coming from a horse in one of the stalls. "Will people believe that story?"

"Whatever my father believes, he is pragmatic man. As long as I am a married woman, he will back my story to sustain the family reputation and will be grateful to Mason." She squeezed his arm. "Someday, when my father dies, perhaps Lin will return and we can find a place where we can live together."

A horse nickered and stomped its hooves in its stall, setting off a wave of unsettled movement among the other animals. Mason's gaze traveled along the twelve stalls, eight occupied, their owners either lodged at a hotel or the horses in need of shoes. The animal smell, ripe with sweat and manure, lay heavy in the air.

Eva straightened her back. "Mason requests permission to leave me, after we are wedded and I have my child. You are here to ask me to give you my lawful husband. As though he's a horse to be traded away once his usefulness is done."

Jillian swallowed a thick lump and nodded. "We need to return home. We don't belong here." She didn't add that it appeared Eva would leave Mason in a flash if Lin returned for her. Pity morphed into contempt.

Eva raised her eyebrows. "My intended has a strange accent, but you do not. Where are you from?"

Mason cleared his throat. This was the moment to be honest, but how would this woman react?

"This will be hard to believe, but we are from a future time," Jillian said. "It's difficult for *me* to accept, but here I am. We are prepared to prove this to you, as best we can."

The other woman made an impatient gesture and stepped away from Mason's touch. "I don't need fantastical lies." Her disappointed gaze settled on him. "Is this why you brought me here? I've already agreed to let you go to her, and bear the shame of abandonment, after you've fulfilled your promise to me. What further humiliation do you require?"

A horse crashed against the side of its stall and Mason's gaze again swept the stable with a frown. He breathed a sigh. "I swear to you, she speaks the truth. But if we are all agreed, perhaps we should plan how I will leave, to provide the best scenario."

Betrayal and hurt showed in Eva's posture and tightness of jaw. "Have you brought your mistress to flaunt before me? You led me to believe there was a vital reason to leave. Instead, you shame me with lies and stories."

The shadow of a man, blurry at the edges, shifted closer, drawing Jillian's attention. "Hello?" she called.

Mason swiveled, his scrutiny following hers. "Did you see someone? There should be no one here."

The shadow remained. Something familiar about the shape and stance awakened her senses. A certainty crashed into her mind. "I know you! From before. You were at the museum."

Mason and Eva squinted, and stared blankly in the same direction, and then exchanged glances.

"My name is Lin," the spectral figure said, the voice muted. "Please help me. Help us."

"Lin," she gasped. "Eva's lover."

Eva whirled with an intake of breath. "Where? Lin! Are you here?"

The man had to be dead in order to appear in this shadowy form. How could Jillian tell this young woman that Lin, standing but a few feet away, was now a ghost?

The spirit drew closer. His form wavered, dark and obscure, in a manner she had never experienced in the past. "You are the only one who sees me," he said. "I am not a real ghost—not dead—yet. Help me."

A shiver climbed Jillian's spine. "Where are you? What is your danger?" A foreboding aura surrounded this disembodied soul. This creature insisted he lived, but then how was his spirit loose from his body?

Eva's eyes rounded and she gripped Mason's forearm. "Who does she speak to?"

"Tell Eva I love her." The figure spoke in a raspy, gravelly voice, as though each word a struggle. "Tell her…you are aware of…hair in a locket." With that, the shadow dissolved.

"Wait!" Had this spirit brought them to his time? But the man was gone. Mouth dry, goosebumps prickling the length of both arms, Jillian swung to face the two. "Lin, or some fragment of him, spoke to me."

Mason's eyebrows lowered as his gaze searched the stables. Understanding dawned in his expression. "Jillian, be very sure. His death will come hard—for everyone."

Eva's voice shook. "What are you two saying? Mason, I'd like to go home. Now. This woman is mad."

Not understanding herself, Jillian shared what the spirit had told her. "You have a locket with a snippet of hair inside?"

Staring at her wide-eyed, Eva clutched something beneath her shirtwaist at chest level. "Lin!" she gasped. "He must be here. No one else knows about my locket."

"You have to believe us, though recent events seem impossible even for me to comprehend," Jillian said. "Give us a chance to explain all to you. Lin—his spirit—was here for a moment. He indicated he is in danger and needs help."

With a small moan, Eva leaned her head against Mason's shoulder. "You brought a witch to me." Her gaze remained locked on Jillian. She made no move to leave. "Tell me then what you will. No living person other than Lin knows about my locket. If you've used witchcraft to speak to him, I don't care. Please tell me where he is."

Jillian shook her head in frustration. Lin's spirit wandered freely from his living body, a situation she had never encountered. "He didn't say where he is. I think he was…retrieved back to his body. He must be ill, perhaps even near death."

Eva gave a strangled scream and sank to the ground. Mason crouched to her side. "Get a cup of water," he ordered, and pointed to a table at the far end of the stable.

Jillian rushed to pour water from a ceramic jug into a dented tin cup. When she returned, Mason's mouth hovered close to Eva's ear, murmuring. He took the cup and helped her take sip after sip.

He glanced up at Jillian, his voice gentle, but slightly chastising. "We easily accept the impossible in our time, with new technologies on the market every year. Life in these times is much the same from birth to death."

Jillian bristled, but realized the veracity of his words. "She asked for the truth," she said, a tinge of sullen in her tone at the sight of Mason's arm around his fiancée. "She can choose to believe us or not."

Eva struggled to her feet and brushed strands of straw off her skirt. She fumbled at the top buttons of her shirtwaist and drew out a tiny gold locket which dangled from a fine chain. "Lin gave this to me as a promise we won't be parted forever." She drew a deep breath before she hid it once more beneath her blouse. "If you lie to me about Lin, I will butcher you and feed you to my father's hogs."

Jillian's eyes widened and she addressed Mason. "I think she can take care of herself just fine."

****

Eva refused to accept their time travel story, with tales of hot water that gushed through pipes into every house, even those of common workers, as well as other greater feats of mankind. She remained unconvinced. Only Jillian's inner sight with Lin appeared to touch Mason's fiancée.

"Tell me what he said, where he is, how he fares,"

the love-stricken woman begged.

Pots must be piled sky-high in the scullery sink at the mansion. Jillian pictured Mrs. March's stormy countenance growing darker by the minute. She forced away the image and tried to focus on Eva. The housekeeper didn't have the ability to help her and Mason return to their own time; Eva *might*.

They sat across from each other on stools in the stable while Mason dealt with a customer at the forge. "This is an unusual case for me. I've been given a gift to see and hear spirits, but Lin isn't dead, or so he says. He appears different from others I've seen. Dark and indistinct, as though he struggles to maintain a form. He said to say he loves you."

Tears welled in Eva's eyes as she leaned forward, gaze riveted on Jillian. "Use your dark arts to call him back. I want to tell him our child will be safe. That I'll wait for him as long as it takes."

Jillian's lips twisted at the term "dark arts," but unbelievers also existed in her own century. "I will try. Most of the time, spirits call to me—not the reverse. Lin has followed me since…" She trailed off. The other woman didn't believe she and Mason hailed from a different era; repeating this point served no purpose. She noticed Lin first in the Crocker house, in its future incarnation as a museum. Her own mind boggled at the complexity of time and space.

"I know what you were about to say," Eva said, as her chin jutted out. "Lin couldn't have been a ghost in some fantastical future. You contradict yourself, since if you insist you are from a distant time, Lin and I would already be in heaven together. He is Chinese and raised in a heathen faith but is now a good Christian man." She sat back and crossed her arms.

"You contradict yourself as well," Jillian shot back, her ire raised. "You believe I speak to spirits but refuse to believe other supernatural occurrences."

They glared at each other. A horse snorted and stomped, as though likewise annoyed at the current situation.

Eva's poise crumpled, her defiant attitude gone. "You said Lin is very ill. I need to get to him." She stood, chest heaving under her white shirtwaist, which was tucked into a light blue skirt. The woman's attire was simple in its lines, a thin ribbon high around her waist with a small bustle gathered and pleated at the back. Yet the cotton was of a fine weave and the cut elegant.

Jillian rose to face her, hands wound in the fabric of her own drab, gray skirt. "He never shared his location."

"Ask him now," Eva ordered, her voice firm.

With a sigh, Jillian closed her eyes. This wouldn't work. Spirits didn't jump at her beck and call. In fact, the situation functioned in reverse. Her head ached with fatigue and stress, and her hands itched, a byproduct of the harsh soap used in the scullery. Now, this young woman before her not only intended to marry Mason but felt comfortable ordering her about.

Lin, she called in her mind, *your bossy girlfriend wants to speak to you.*

The heavy odor of large animals made her nostrils twitch. Leather tackle and saddles, stained with sweat and hung on racks, added to the steamy atmosphere. The rumble of carts on the dirt street cast up dust and voices drifted in from passersby. No shadow crossed her eyelids; no voice spoke in her ear.

She had a few frank questions of her own for Lin, who first appeared in her modern era. He appeared to be the key to this peculiar chapter in her life and had dragged her and Mason back in time to do his bidding. The man, near death or not, had a lot to answer for.

"What does he say?" The other woman's question interrupted her ruminations.

Jillian opened her eyes and shook her head. "Nothing, I'm afraid. He comes and goes. I don't have control over when he appears."

Eva's lips twisted in doubt, but a tinge of hope remained in her eyes. "You must find out where he is as soon as possible." She glanced around, fingers knotted. "You live at the Crocker house as a maid. Has he shown himself to you there?"

In the future. "At times, but today is the first he's spoken to me. Perhaps because you are here."

Eva's chagrin mirrored her own at being tied together in this manner. "We must figure a way to meet, as often as possible," she said. "This evening, tomorrow morning, before it's too late."

Eva, Mason, Lin, and herself, all linked. This was to be a *ménage a quatre.*

****

Jillian trudged back to the Crocker mansion, the one place where she belonged in this century. As she approached the tall white house, with its numerous narrow Italianate arches and neatly trimmed trees set in an expansive lawn, her steps slowed. The trio of structures—mansion, servants' house and grand gallery—lined up in a row, a statement of respectability and wealth.

Zeb knelt over his work at the base of a tree, and Caleb's skinny arms opened and closed broad shears to clip the grass. Child labor laws didn't exist yet. She knew all across the nation, children slaved under horrendous conditions. Caleb's situation was an easy one compared to many.

No wonder most people died before age sixty, especially those in the working classes. For herself, dishes heaped higher in the sink, and myriad other chores waited her return. A long afternoon of physical labor stretched out before her; toil and slog until her back ached and all she wanted to do was lay down on her narrow cot in exhaustion. And this was after a brief taste of this life; weeks, months, and years promised to make her haggard by forty.

Who could say when or if Lin would appear to her again? For months, she would need to appease the Crockers' housekeeper while Mason fulfilled his obligation to Eva. Then, and only then, might they seek to return to their own time. She rounded the back of the servants' quarters to the back steps. The aroma of biscuits filled her mouth with saliva. Perhaps Mrs. Stevens would let her have one biscuit before she settled into the scullery.

The cook, rolling out pie dough on the table, cast a wary glance as she entered. The other maid, Sarah, about to lift a bucket of hot water off the stove, gave her a grim smile and hurried out of the kitchen.

"I'll get started on the dishes. I'm sure there are plenty," Jillian said, relieved March was nowhere in sight. Hopefully the housekeeper stayed busy with Mr. Crocker's care and hadn't yet been downstairs.

Mrs. Stevens cleared her throat and continued with

her task. "I don't make the decisions around here."

A small thud drew Jillian's gaze. March stood in the doorway in a dark dress somewhat crumpled, eyebrows lowered and mouth downturned. Behind her, Sarah lurked, eyes glued to the scene that unfolded. The housekeeper's narrow face sagged with fatigue and lines etched deep into the corners of her mouth. At her feet lay a fabric sack.

"Mrs. March, I know I shouldn't have left," Jillian said before the housekeeper berated her. "This truly was an emergency. I'll get right to work. I promise to finish all my duties." She moved forward, with hopes to skirt by the woman before she launched a verbal attack. The day had already been stressful enough without one of March's famous rebukes.

"Stop right there, young madam." The stern tone brooked no debate. "Not one more step into this house."

Jillian obeyed with sigh. She would have to undergo a tongue lashing as a punishment for skipping out on her duties once again. She bowed her head in what she hoped to be a penitent posture.

The admonishment didn't take long.

"In all my born days, I haven't come across one like you. Some people cannot be saved from themselves." March held out an envelope. "Here are your wages. The clothes you arrived in are in the bag. You are dismissed."

Chapter Twelve

Jillian froze. Her mind spun in an attempt to process this latest turn of events. March's severe expression shot nuclear warheads in her direction, while Sarah's eyes gleamed with a look of satisfaction. Mrs. Stevens' broad back remained hunched over the dough. This house was key to her return to her time; she couldn't lose access to the dining room that seemed to be a portal.

"You can't throw me out. I can't leave this house. I haven't—"

"It is not for you to tell me what I can and cannot do." Mrs. March drew up her shoulders, her back ramrod straight. "Please remove yourself straightaway. I will not ask you to wear your indecent clothing out of this house, but the uniform is the property of the Crockers. Return it by the end of the week."

Why didn't the cook intercede on her behalf? Mrs. Stevens liked her and might vouch for her if only she would speak up. Emily too, and Caleb and Zeb. Not Sarah, but you couldn't please everyone. A few voices on her behalf, even one, might help.

The housekeeper took a step toward her. One foot nudged the bag of clothes as if it contained snakes. "Out with you. No need for dramatics."

Mrs. Stevens had paused in her work, but didn't look up. There would be no help from her.

"I have nowhere to go." Jillian's voice shook as the realization dawned on her again that she was homeless, jobless, and without skills useful in this century.

"You should return to your father's house and stop this unchaste pursuit of your errant fiancé," Mrs. March said. "You are not the first girl to be deceived by a man." She prodded the bag forward with a small kick. "Take your belongings and leave."

There was no further use in pleading her case. The housekeeper stood stiff as a stone wall. Jillian grabbed the bag and stumbled out the kitchen door. Which way should she go now? Back to Mason, who had resolved to marry a desirable young woman?

Her thin wage envelope contained three fifty-cent coins. All those dishes scrubbed, rooms dusted, floors swept; so much work resulted in this paltry sum, not enough for a room and meal for one night. Truth be told, Mrs. March had been generous since she hadn't worked more than three full days.

Shame flooded her at the need to beg help from Mason. He'd fought his own way through this century, suffered much, and come out ahead. The situation was very different for a woman. She might offer herself as a maid, but she had no reference. She glanced over her shoulder at the grand mansion, its doors now shut firm against her. The place had offered sanctuary, room and board, and she'd let it slip away.

This is Lin and Eva's fault. Those star-crossed lovers don't care who they hurt as long as they are reunited.

For years, compassion drove her to communicate with spirits, to be their conduit to share their stories with her readers. The loss of her mother and brother,

Garrett, when she was eight years old drove her to help those wandering the in-between world of living and dead. Someday, she would receive a message from her mother or brother; those little-girl hurts of loss and emptiness bored a hole in her heart.

She'd seen and spoken to dozens of ghosts over the past two decades. This time was different. Certainly, danger had stalked her before, but never had a spirit upended her life in such an all-encompassing way—not even close. Her desire to help Lin, therefore, was muted. If Mason wasn't so chivalrous, she would drag him into the Crockers' dining room and back to the twenty-first century.

"Jane!"

She whirled to see Caleb approach her at a trot, his young face anxious. "March was hopping mad when you went missing," he said, breathless as he halted. "She gave you the boot, didn't she?"

Jillian nodded and lifted her bag. "All I have in the world. My clothes and three fifty-cent pieces. Any suggestions where I might find another job?"

"Not as good as the one you've lost. You really should have worked harder." The boy grimaced and shoved grass-stained hands into his pockets. "You had food and a room."

"Okay. I get it, I blew it."

His brow furrowed. "You blew on what?"

"Just an expression. It means I'm at fault." Zeb's tall frame rounded the corner, but he didn't come nearer. "I suppose I'd better let you get back to your chores before March fires you, too."

"*Fires* me?" He broke into a laugh. "She's ornery, but she'd never set me on fire. Gosh, I'll miss you."

"Yeah, me too." Jillian faced the town, her lone option as farmland, open range, and the river spread out in the other directions. "Goodbye, Caleb." She took a few steps before a thought struck her. "Hey, may I ask a favor?"

"Sure, but what can I do?"

She approached him once more. "I plan to come back, one day soon, and I need you to let me into the house."

His eyes widened and he took a step back. "Uh, no. I'd lose my job if March caught you inside again. What do you want inside the mansion?" His voice lowered almost to a whisper. "Are you going to steal the silver?"

"No, of course not." She twisted her lips as she quickly considered an answer. "I left a valuable item of mine in the house. I, uh, hid it so no one would find it. I want to leave this item where it's hidden for now, in a safe spot, but sometime soon I'll want to retrieve it."

His face brightened at this explanation. "You wouldn't have to go inside at all. I'd fetch it for you anytime you like."

That didn't work at all, since the item she desired was access to the time portal. But she couldn't tell the boy the real reason. "Maybe," she hedged. "Remember, though, I'll be back to see you."

The boy smiled, his face open and affable. "Sure. Good luck, Jane."

"One more thing, Caleb. My name is Jillian."

****

This time the town took on a more intimidating appearance. If not accompanied by a man, women paraded in pairs, never alone. Men gaped at her in open appreciation, perhaps emboldened by her plain and

121

lowly dress. One of them offered her "two bits" for a cuddle. She took firm steps, recalling modern advice to not appear a victim which might make her a target by unsavory sorts. She mustn't appear to be a woman without a livelihood or home—or most important in these times, a male protector. There was Mason, but they couldn't claim each other publicly. What rationale could he offer to the world if he provided shelter and food? People would assume she was his mistress, and the shame would ripple out to Eva. Even if the other woman annoyed her, it still wasn't right to subject her to humiliation. Eva's father could even halt the wedding, and then Mason might blame her for her interference.

And the damned hammers never stopped! The pounding from construction thudded into her brain from every direction and worsened her anxiety. She veered off onto a street she hadn't been on before, lined with brick edifices and no new construction under way. A young boy in ragged pants raced past, followed by two more in similarly drab attire. They hooted and hollered as they ran. Horses lined up in front of buildings, tied to horizontal posts.

The aroma of fried meat awakened her hunger and drew her to a doorway. From inside sounded the clink of glasses, piano music, and the laughter of a woman. A sign confirmed this was indeed a saloon named *Lou's*. Her stomach rumbled; she opened the door.

Jillian stopped inside as the door swung shut, unable to see while her eyes adjusted to the darkened room. The music tinkled and men's deep voices boomed. Cigar smoke mixed with the aroma of food. Gradually, the saloon came into view: a huge horseshoe-shaped bar in the middle of the room, surrounded by tables and a few discreet booths in the corners. Although not even noon, the saloon was full.

"You'll attract plenty of mashers if you're not careful." A middle-aged woman approached her, clad in ruby satin that matched her hair, with a corset peeking from under a purple feathered boa.

"Masher?"

"Fella on the make. Unless that's what you're hopeful for. For that, you have to check in with the owner." The woman grinned from some inside joke and assessed her. "New in town?"

If only you knew. "Just this week," she admitted.

"Gal like you could do well for herself here. Men like your sort as much as ones like me." She adjusted her corset, which thrust her fleshy bosom dangerously higher. "You'd remind them of the girl they left back home. Not in that dreary dress though. We'd find an outfit more suitable, more colorful."

The bartender set a steaming plate of bacon and eggs before a large man at the bar in front of her. Five slices of bacon disappeared into the man's mouth, one after another. She swallowed drily when he did.

"I'm Louella, but everyone calls me Lou. What brings you to my establishment?"

A real-live Wild West madam. Just like the spirit she intended to visit in Virginia City. The irony rolled over her but didn't amuse her. Worry and a ravenous appetite intervened.

"Can I get some food to go...to, um, eat somewhere else?" Fifty cents must have some purchasing power, with wages so low. It had to be enough for a meal. She couldn't face Mason while both hungry and bereft of a place to stay.

The woman's eyebrows lowered and she appeared on the verge of kicking Jillian out the door. "My food's good enough for you, but my place isn't?"

She swallowed. A handful of men, rough looking in their appearance, stared from a nearby table. "I don't seek the attention of gentlemen. If you understand what I mean."

The woman chuckled, and the laugh set her bosom atremble. "I understand plenty. I don't believe there are any *gentlemen* present." She chuckled again. "Tell you what, sit with me at my table and I'll keep the mashers away while you eat. Who knows, maybe you'll decide to stay awhile. Money's good here, and plenty of it."

No harm could come to her if this confident woman sat next to her. Once fed, she'd go straight to Mason. "I can afford fifty cents for a meal, no more."

Lou's assessing gaze made Jillian feel like a heifer at auction. "You *are* new to town, aren't you? I charge fifteen cents for a full breakfast. Tell you what, the meal's on me. Let's call it a business expense."

A maid or a prostitute. So far, her options in the nineteenth century weren't promising. Perhaps this woman knew of another type of job, one she could do on her feet and with her clothes on. She followed Lou to a corner booth and a man with a well-waxed handlebar mustache scurried up as soon as they sat.

"Two flapjack specials and two whiskeys," Lou ordered.

"Just a water for me," Jillian added.

"*Two* whiskeys," the madam repeated, and the man headed to the kitchen doors.

No matter, no one insisted she had to drink alcohol.

Her stomach rumbled, a long loud complaint that Jillian hoped the other woman didn't hear.

"Usual rate on this new one?" A scraggly bearded man loomed over Jillian with a leer. His unwashed stench made her eyes water.

Lou waved a hand in a shooing motion. "Not for sale at the moment. Can't you see we're conferring."

"Put me first on the lineup, Lou. This one's nice and clean."

The madam half rose from the table, one hand clenched. "You saying my girls ain't clean?"

He edged backward. "I always come here, don't I? You should treat your regulars with more respect."

Jillian regretted the decision to enter the saloon. She'd been inside the doors for less than five minutes, was being interviewed for a job as a prostitute, and had already created a minor disturbance.

"Sit at the bar and buy a round for the room. Then maybe I'll forgive you." The woman gave him a stiff-lipped grin and he stomped to the bar. Within seconds, the barman poured out a line of whiskeys and young women in elaborate costumes hustled around the room to deliver them.

"Nicely handled," Jillian said, impressed by Lou's cool self-assurance. She had defused the man's insistence and made money on the deal too. "This is your place?"

"For the last ten years. I worked here for twelve years before that, saved almost every penny." She lifted her chin. "I run a good establishment, but I have rules. Men like discipline, even if they tell you they don't. They're children who want to be guided."

Two giant plates of flapjacks, eggs, and ham slabs

landed on the table, followed by two whiskeys. For several minutes, Jillian thought of nothing but the meal in front of her. Lou knocked back her whiskey in one swallow and nibbled at the food.

"Girls always want to tell me their story before we talk business. So, let's hear yours."

Jillian's hunger eased as the pancakes disappeared and she started in on the eggs. The over-salted meal stimulated her thirst and she eyed the whiskey. A bad idea. She pondered Lou's question. What difference did it make if she told this woman the truth? She'd never step inside this bordello again.

She took a deep breath and sat back against the plush cushioned booth. "I have a gift for talking to spirits. Ever since I was a child. I ran a business where I traveled and wrote about my experiences. Lately—" she shook her head "—everything's been flipped upside down in my life."

Setting aside her fork, Lou leaned forward. "You're a clairvoyant?"

"In a way, I suppose. I don't call spirits from the grave. I see the ones who remain here, caught unseen in our world. I tell their stories."

Lou's gaze drifted across her saloon, her bottom lip caught between her teeth. Two men swung open the door and made for the bar. Two women sidled to their sides in a moment. Four glasses of amber colored liquid clinked on the bar the next moment. Like a smoothly oiled machine.

"I might have use for a girl like you," the madam said, offering Jillian an assessing look. "There's money to be made with this gift of yours—whether you're telling the truth or not. Men have needs other than drinking and whoring. Spiritual needs." She slapped the table with the palm of her hand and laughed. "Lou serves up spirits and spirits, that's what they'll say. I could be famous for this."

Was she being offered a job? "Um, I'm not sure—"

"Make it sound good…believable…whatever you tell them. I set the fee. You keep the tips, and men tip better when they're satisfied. I should know."

The door opened again, and another man strode in. The piano man launched into another merry tune. Lou's saloon didn't hurt for customers.

Was she really considering this? "Just so I understand. I would be a clairvoyant, nothing more."

Lou pointed across the room. "I'll set you up in a booth. The men pay me, then I send them over to you." She wagged her chin at the empty plate. "You arrived as starved as an alley cat, so I figure you need the work. I can feed you two meals a day."

A clairvoyant. She had never sold her services in this manner, but what other skills did she possess? One of the prostitutes led a customer up the stairs, which gave Jillian an idea. "I need a place to stay, too."

The madam chuckled. "You drive a hard bargain, but if there's one thing I'm not short on, it's beds and rooms."

They shook hands across the table. Jillian tucked away any misgivings about the venture. The madam offered room, board, and protection against being cast out on the streets.

Lou raised a hand and hollered, "Two more whiskeys over here."

Chapter Thirteen

Jillian sauntered toward the forge, her immediate troubles taken care of: hunger sated, a job secured, and a place to stay. Tonight, she would hold court as a mystic in one of Lou's private booths in exchange for room, board, and tips. She warned the madam one more time that her body wasn't for sale and some clients might misunderstand and leave unsatisfied with the outcome of their session. Lou simply shrugged with a smug smile on her lips. Jillian had the feeling the madam believed she would eventually become one of the saloon's regular whores.

Time. She needed time to figure out how to return. If she had to be a clairvoyant in a saloon in order to survive, she resolved to give it her best.

Now, the sounds of construction didn't bother her; the reverberations kept pace with her heightened pulse. Dark gray clouds crossed the warm midday sun and provided a welcome shadow. One large cloud resembled a bus, another an airplane. Wishful thinking, she mused. Perspiration under her arms dampened her blouse and she wished for the freedom of capris and sandals. Instead, heavy skirts constrained her stride and, along with her long-sleeved blouse, conspired to hold in the heat and make her uncomfortable.

Ridiculous, not having phones. No texting or email. No video calls. To speak to Mason, she had to hoof it along the streets and see him face-to-face. If he wasn't at the forge, and no one near enlightened her as to his whereabouts, then her trip would be pointless, and another excursion required later. So much wasted time in the past. It didn't matter if she had knowledge of future technology when she didn't know how to invent any of the forthcoming wonders.

Jillian's pace increased as she neared the forge, and a few sprinkles of rain dampened the street dust. A breeze gusted, and a playbill sailed across her path. Darker clouds roiled in the western sky. A memory of the murky river, already full at its banks, flickered through her mind. Then the forge stood before her and Mason filled her mind.

Heat rippled from the broad open doorway. She hesitated at the entrance, her throat tight at this view of the man she loved. Mason's massive arms glistened with sweat as he struck the glowing-red metal over and over with a sledgehammer. The strikes rang and blocked the sound of her voice, and so she watched and waited while he labored. His focus remained riveted on his work. He bent the metal into place, heated it anew in the fire and hammered some more, his actions concise and deliberate, a master at his trade. At last, he thrust the completed horseshoe into a bucket of water and looked up.

"Jillian."

The one word echoed all the feelings she carried for him in her heart. Yes, she would stay in this century if he asked it of her. A modern life without him would be void of happiness. They belonged to each other, regardless of time and place. He ripped off his heavy gloves and grasped her arm. In a flash, he had pulled her inside and out of sight of the street. One arm around her waist, he bent her to him and kissed her deeply. The scent of his sweat blended with the earthy, metallic smells in the forge.

She stepped back and laughed, her heart light as she ran a hand down the front of her dress. "Oh no. I'm a mess." Dark streaks from Mason's blacksmith apron marred her gray blouse and skirt. The outfit needed to be laundered before she returned it to March.

His gaze flickered to the doorway. "What brings you back so soon? Not that I mind, but won't you be missed at the mansion?"

A frisson of annoyance rippled through her. Was he concerned someone might see them together? "I've been fired from that job and hired for another this morning. Actually, I've gone into business for myself."

His brow furrowed as she spoke. "You've been fired? Because of me and your visit here earlier?"

Jillian shrugged. "Doesn't matter. I've been hired as a clairvoyant with my own booth at Lou's saloon. With room and board provided, it's my best option for the moment. I wanted you to know where I'll be."

He stepped back. "Lou's! You can't. That's a bordello. Why were you even there?"

Her tone hardened. "I'm not selling my body. Lou will promote me as a mystic, someone who can connect her customers with their deceased loved ones."

"I thought you didn't do personal readings."

"I thought you didn't know how to shoe horses," she shot back. "Both of us need to make our way in this century." She raised her eyebrows. "Anyway, how are you familiar with Lou's?"

He looked abashed. "The place is a saloon first,

bordello second. There isn't a bar in town that doesn't have that particular secondary business. There must be dozens of them. They're rough places for women not in the trade."

"I'll manage," she said in a cool tone. "It'll give me a job to do and sustain me while you're on your honeymoon." The words sprang from her mouth as though from another person. Where had this new petulance come from?

His jaw clenched. "This isn't the twenty-first century, Jillian. The laws won't protect a woman who works in a place like that. If you were assaulted, they'd say you asked for it."

A twinge of doubt rippled through her at the truth in his words. She was a fish out of water in these times. She straightened her shoulders and pretended a confidence she didn't feel. "I came by to let you know where I'll be. Right now, I need to buy some clothes for my debut as a clairvoyant."

"Jillian, wait. We can think of another option."

Mason's disapproval and warnings prickled. Without another word, she stomped out of the forge. He might have congratulated her on being resourceful. No longer would she let events dictate her life. From now on, she must take charge of her destiny. She needed clothes and then to find Lin and, somehow, reunite him with Eva. Then, she would fetch Mason and transport them from this bloody place.

****

Her mind swirled with regrets as she searched for a dressmaker's shop. She had risen to anger too quickly at the forge. Her nerves prickled, temper short, and emotions close to the surface. In the reflection of a shop window stood a slight blonde woman, pale with worried eyes, in a dull gray skirt that didn't fit well. *Is that me? Am I still me?*

She continued to scan storefronts, but there were no department stores or boutiques. Off-the-rack dresses didn't exist in this era, did they? How in the world was she supposed to return her maid uniform to Mrs. March by the end of the week? Fabrics were easy enough to find in any general store, but she didn't know how to sew anything more complicated than a loose button. After walking up one street and down another, a small sign appeared that indicated a seamstress worked within.

Jillian entered the cool interior, well-lit from a large front window. A dressmaker's dummy clad with a simple calico dress stood in the center of the tidy room.

"May I help you?" A soft voice drew Jillian's attention to a doorway at the back. A tall slender woman, mousy brown hair piled on her head making her appear even taller, paused before she approached. Her teal dress gathered in pretty pleats at the hips and swept back to a small bustle.

"I need someone who can make a dress or two for me, as soon as possible. Today," Jillian added. "Is that doable?"

The woman's mouth quirked. "A dress in a day?"

Jillian gestured at her own apparel. "This belongs to my former employer and it's all I have."

The seamstress' face relaxed into a quizzical smile. "You have no clothes at all? That's a problem indeed."

"Yes. A long story." Jillian nodded toward the simple navy and cream calico attire on the dummy. "Perhaps you have an outfit already made that I could purchase. I'm not choosy."

The woman crossed to the dummy and fingered the material on the long sleeves. "One of my first creations. I always liked it, but the customer died of fever before she picked it up. I planned to rework the neckline a bit higher in this year's fashion."

"I don't need fashionable," Jillian broke in. "Just serviceable. May I ask the price? And whether you might fit it for me today?"

A small smoky gray cat strolled into the room from the back and rubbed itself against the bottom of Jillian's skirt. Its contented purr brought a smile to her lips. She bent to stroke its lean back. "What a sweetie you are," she murmured.

"I believe Anabelle wants me to say yes," the woman said. "In particular for a woman with no other clothes to wear. I suppose I could make the time." She took a deep breath and let it go. "I'm Catherine Scott."

"Jillian Winchester."

Anabelle gave a soft meow as though she, too, offered an introduction, and they laughed.

Catherine began unbuttoning the outfit from the figure. "Well, Jillian, let's go into the other room and take some measurements. You're of similar stature to the woman I made this for, so it shouldn't need much alteration. I'd be pleased to see it worn."

The dressmaker worked efficiently. She jotted down measurements, asked Jillian to try on the already-made dress, and then set a dozen pins into place. "A new hemline, the shoulders let out a touch, and it'll do. I can have it for you by the end of the day. A second dress will take a few days, I'm afraid. I'm quick, but there's just one of me."

"I can't thank you enough."

"The second dress ought to be more fashionable, I think. I have some lovely lace and ribbons." Catherine's expression was hopeful. "I have an emerald taffeta that would complement the color of your eyes."

"My needs are simple, and my means are, er, reduced. Whatever cotton material you have on hand will do."

The dressmaker smiled. "I have just the thing. I bought a mustard yellow and gray calico at a discount so I can offer you a good price."

After they settled upon a price for the two dresses and a set of underclothes, Jillian left with the impression they could become friends if she stayed in this century. She almost sighed in relief at the affordable cost of the clothes, which Catherine said she could pay for when all items were completed. How trusting shopkeepers in this time were, to allow credit to a stranger, based on instinct.

She needed to be successful at her new venture as a mystic. Even with room and board covered, she already had debts to pay.

Back on the street, the sun's halo shone through the gray clouds directly overhead, the rain at bay for now. Without her cellphone, which she had always used as a substitute for a watch, she had no idea of the exact time anymore. Still, she had hours before her stint at Lou's saloon. Time enough to visit Eva and get more information about Lin.

According to Mason, his fiancée lived in a neighborhood called Alkali Flats where many wealthy families lived. The area wasn't very far away, but her feet already ached, and blisters had formed on both heels. A horse or cart would be handy—really, a car even better—but since she had none of these, there was naught to do but ignore the blisters and march forward.

After asking for directions twice, she arrived in the elegant neighborhood. Tall, narrow Victorian homes lined the wide street, with larger mansions holding court at the corners. Two jet-black horses pulled a carriage, the clip-clop of their hooves a gentle music compared to the hustle of the town.

"Excuse me." She stopped before a child, perhaps eight or nine years old, sitting on a stoop, a book upon her lap. "Do you know where the McAlisters live?"

The girl's hazel eyes lit up. Light brown ringlets framed her face. "Of course. I know where everyone lives. The Parkers live in the house across the street, the Evans in the yellow house over there, the Daniels next door. My best friend, Lizzie, lives in the big white house on the corner. I'm waiting for her to come and play with me. She has a new doll with blonde hair like yours."

"Sounds like you have a very good friend. The McAlisters?"

The girl cocked her head and her curls bounced. "Are you a maid? Your dress is dirty."

Jillian glanced down at the front of her shirtwaist and skirt, smudged from Mason's embrace. "I'm having a new one made at this very moment and will have this one cleaned." A thought occurred to her. "Do you know where there's a laundry?"

She wrinkled her nose. "The Chinese do laundry. Their area is over there." She waved a hand toward the west. "I don't go there. Mother says the Chinese steal children and sell them as slaves."

This was how prejudice jumped from generation to generation. Jillian couldn't help commenting. "They're no more likely to kidnap you than anyone else. I'm sure they're too busy with their own affairs."

The girl's chin tilted up in a haughty manner as she plucked at the ruffles on her skirt. "The McAlisters live in the next block, the blue house with the stone lions out front." She bent her head and resumed reading.

Jillian sighed and trudged forward. A wetness at her heel indicated a blister had popped. The raw sore gave her a slight limp. A shiny carriage drawn by two well-groomed horses clattered by, and she glimpsed two ladies inside, their large hats filling the interior. Laughter emanated from the coach, a carefree sound that made Jillian feel somewhat sorry for herself.

The turquoise Victorian towered above the street, not quite a mansion, but near enough to be impressive just the same. The two stone lions perched before the entryway, as though to guard against riffraff like Jillian in her bedraggled maid uniform and bloody heel. Would she even be granted admittance? She hesitated and considered whether the servants' entrance might be more appropriate. But no, she meant to speak to the daughter of the house. She marched up the steps, past the lions, and rapped on the door.

A small man, not much more than five feet tall, swung the door open. His dark brown eyes took in her situation in life with one swift glance. "Around the back, if you will."

The door began to close and Jillian blocked it with one hand. "I'm here to see Eva. I'm a...a friend. Tell her Jillian is here. She will want to see me."

The opening widened and the man's eyebrows

arched as he frowned at her. "I'm absolutely certain you are not an acquaintance of Miss McAlister. Please remove your hand."

She drew back her shoulders and kept her hand braced against the door. The lions had nothing on this man. "Eva will want to see me. I'm *absolutely certain* of that. She will be very displeased to learn you turned me away." Her heart thudded against her chest. After traveling all this way, she refused to leave without speaking to Mason's fiancée.

"Wait here," the man said, and then peered at the neighbors' houses on all sides. "No, not at the door." He pointed toward the walkway next to the street. "Go over there. I'll fetch you if you're admitted." His tone indicated this was doubtful. He shoved the door closed, sending Jillian backward a couple of paces.

Reluctantly, she obeyed, aware of the lions' superior eyes on her back as she retreated. The butler didn't make her wait long, however. This time he opened the door wide, as though he welcomed her, but puzzlement reflected in his eyes.

"You may come in." He craned his neck out the door in one direction, then the other. "Be quick."

Jillian didn't care if he considered her appearance an embarrassment to his dignity. She strode into the cool, dim interior, and wondered what new challenges the day might present.

Chapter Fourteen

The diminutive butler led the way into a parlor, his disdainful attitude and impeccable attire making up for his height—or lack of it.

"Don't touch anything," he ordered, with another hard stare at her smudged shirtwaist. "Miss McAlister will be with you presently."

"I'm here." Breathless, Eva brushed past him. "This woman is here to, uh—" She fumbled for words. "—seek assistance for the Children's Home. We aren't to be disturbed." She shut the parlor doors and whirled around to face Jillian. "Do you have news? Have you found him? Is he ill?"

Tired from the walk and of being looked down upon, she bristled. "I've been busy with other matters. Already today, I've lost one job and had to find another—which is of more importance to me because I arrived here with nothing. I must feed, clothe, and house myself, or starve on the streets. As a favor to you, I've walked all the way here and my feet *hurt*." The complaint flew out of her mouth and she almost cringed. The nineteenth century had crushed her usual tranquil demeanor.

Eva's eyes grew round, and she looked somewhat chagrined. "Please, sit down already." She gestured to the sofa.

"Thank you, how kind." Jillian sank with a sigh

onto the soft cushion. Guilt flooded her for her sharp words; the woman had lost her lover and her secret pregnancy would soon be evident. They each had what seemed to be unsurmountable problems. "Perhaps we can help each other."

Eva crossed the room and tugged a braided rope. She then sat stiffly on an inlaid-wood chair covered in rose-colored fabric. Her hands fiddled with her skirts. A slight tic twitched at the corner of one eye. "How much? I have some jewelry, but Papa doesn't give me an allowance."

"I'm not here for payment." Jillian wrinkled her forehead. "Not money, in any case. I believe Lin brought me to this era, Mason as well. If I help you find Lin, can you promise to help us return to our time?"

Eva's lips twisted. "Your time travel story."

Tucking her chin, Jillian waited. She refused to explain her account again.

A tidy maid peeped at them from the doorway, her black dress covered in front with a white bib apron, and a small white cap sat atop curly auburn hair.

"Refreshments for my guest," Eva ordered, and the maid withdrew. Her gaze drifted to the window. "I don't know what to believe anymore. I was raised to believe I had one path in life, marriage to a man of my station, and a houseful of children. I stepped off that path, and now my entire world is in confusion. I doubt you'd understand." She gestured to Jillian. "If Papa witnessed me in our front salon with a maid, offering refreshments, and you...like that..." Her words trailed off.

"No offense taken," Jillian said through gritted teeth, her ire raised despite her earlier resolve. "So, do you agree to help or not? I have a mile hike in front of me, and my feet are a mess. I don't suppose you have a couple of Band-Aids?"

Eva gave her a blank stare.

"An amenity of the future," she clarified. "Never mind about my feet."

"I agree to provide assistance, although I haven't a clue what you believe I can do. First, however, you must fulfill your promise."

Jillian heaved a heavy sigh and leaned forward. "Okay. Tell me all you know about Lin."

A smile softened Eva's mouth. "He's tall, taller than Mason, and slender. But very strong. His hands—"

"Not his sex appeal," Jillian interrupted with a roll of her eyes. "I get that you were attracted, or there wouldn't be a little Lin on its way. I want to know what he does, where he lives, and whether he has enemies who wish him harm."

The maid entered, carrying a tray topped with a pitcher, glasses, and slices of brown cake. "Cider cake, Miss, and lemonade."

"That's fine. Leave the tray, Patience. I can serve."

The maid darted a glance at her mistress' unusual guest. She pursed her lips before she hurried away. Eva thrust a glass of lemonade and slice of cake at Jillian. "His family owns a tailor shop in the Chinese area. Lin worked there with his two brothers. All three of them lived above the shop. He got along with everyone I suppose."

"Have you been to the tailor's shop?"

Eva tilted her head to one side and spoke as if explaining something simple to a child. "A respectable white woman doesn't go into that side of town." She brushed a cake crumb from her skirt. "My brother, Ernest, went in my stead. Lin's brothers said they haven't seen him for weeks."

Jillian frowned. "Is it possible your father knows about you and Lin and is responsible for his disappearance?"

Eva bit her lip. "He hasn't spoken of it to me. But you said he's alive, near death." The young woman's face crumpled. "Where is he?"

The cider used in the cake was strong and the tang of it mixed pleasantly with the sweet, chewy texture. "I'd like to talk to Lin's brothers. His spirit may approach me there."

"He's not...here, now?"

Jillian peered about the room, casting her unique abilities to sense abnormal presences to all corners of the parlor. "He's never been here," she said after a few moments. "Perhaps his energy, if he's in a weakened state, can't travel this far. Is the area where Chinese live and work near the forge where I spotted him this morning?

"Very close, yes." She fingered the locket under her shirtwaist. "But his brothers have had no word from him."

"I'll need the name of the tailor shop so I can make my own inquiries. His spirit may contact me there. Believe me, if Lin is able to get me—and Mason— home again, I'm very motivated to find him."

Eva's hand trembled as she sipped her lemonade. She put the cup on the tray and took a deep breath. "If you don't, Mason takes me to the altar on Saturday. He's a handsome enough man, though not at all like Lin." Her eyes narrowed. "Mason will never abandon me to a life of shame. If I don't get my man, you'll never get yours."

****

Despite Eva's obnoxious attitude, she at least had the grace to order a carriage to convey Jillian back to the dress shop. The self-absorbed young woman hadn't displayed the slightest curiosity where Jillian would go next, without a job or place to stay. She hadn't volunteered the facts of her new situation. There was no point in handing Mason's fiancée another excuse to be unpleasant with details about her job at Lou's and the room above the saloon.

The wind had picked up and a light rain fell, another reason to be grateful for the ride into town. The handsome coachman, a strapping fellow in his thirties, handed her down at the dress shop as though he assisted a great lady and not a bedraggled maid. Not everyone was a snob.

He held an umbrella over her. "Any packages for me to carry?"

"I'm sure I can manage but thank you. I'll be quick." She hurried inside.

"Ah," Catherine said, as she emerged from the back room. "Just in time. Your dress is ready. I've selected a pattern and trimmings for your next one. Would you like to see them?"

Jillian shook her head. "I trust your judgment, and I'm afraid I'm out of time today. May I change here?"

The dressmaker's gaze lifted to the window to where the carriage and driver waited. "You *are* a woman of mystery. No clothes to your name, but a fine carriage at the door. Someday I hope to hear your story."

Jillian struggled into the uncomfortable corset which pinched her middle and settled the navy and cream calico dress over her shoulders. Her appearance in the mirror was agreeable, no longer a servant to be bossed around but an ordinary woman of the 1870s. Catherine helped her with the buttons, far too many of them for Jillian's taste. She added zippers to the long list of inventions she missed. If all failed, could she really stay and make a life here? Yes, she determined. Mason wanted her as much as she wanted him. That had to be enough.

As Catherine wrapped up the maid uniform in brown paper tied with twine, she chatted about the changes to the city: its surge in population since the discovery of gold, the laying of wooden-block pavements and cobblestone streets, and the fresh increase of the male population after the end of the war between the states. Annabelle purred from a chair, overseeing events like a queen upon a throne.

"Thank you, and I'll be back for the other dress on Saturday." Jillian hesitated; if all went well, she would never be back. She couldn't skip town without payment. One way or another, she needed to settle this debt. "You've been very kind. I'll make sure you're paid in full."

Catherine's face lit up in pleasure. "I knew you'd be a good customer the moment Annabelle took a shine to you. She's never wrong."

They parted, with Jillian half-regretting that she might never see the congenial woman again. The coachman gave her a grin of approval when she emerged from the shop.

"I'd like to be dropped off at Lou's saloon," she

said as he opened the carriage door for her. "Do you know where that is?"

His face broke into a smile and he chuckled. "I've been known to stop by, but never during work hours."

"I guess there's a first time for everything." She hopped into the carriage, and they set off.

****

A line of men waited while Jillian settled herself in a dark booth in one corner at Lou's. The piano jangled a tune, and a buzz of deep voices filled the room while the smells of dirty bodies, perfume, and cigar smoke blended into an odiferous soup. Young women clad in bright-colored satin and feathers served drinks. Men darted glances her way, clearly curious about the hand-lettered sign on the table: *Clairvoyant session, $1.* A hefty price. Across the saloon, holding court in her own booth, Lou collected the fees with a Cheshire cat grin. Jillian fingered her skirts, nervous about this new venture and what the men expected for their money.

The first customer, a sallow-cheeked man whose hair appeared left unwashed for years, sat on the edge of his seat, as far from her as possible. He leaned forward and spoke in a raspy whisper. "I'd like to hit it big in the goldfield, quick as you say where to go. I have kinfolk back home in Ohio who need the money."

The man believed her some type of oracle, spouting answers to all questions. "I can't help you find your gold." At his side, the faint outline of a woman flashed then disappeared. Whom had he abandoned in order to seek a fortune? She took a stab at it. "Your family misses you. Perhaps once you had a wife?"

His eyes narrowed. "I ain't never got a wife. Someone telling you lies?" He peered around the saloon as if ready to throw a fist or two. "I put down a dollar to sit with you here." He pushed a scrap of paper in front of her, a rudimentary map drawn by an unsteady hand. "Just point to where, that's all I need."

Jillian shook her head quickly and sought to appease him. "I can only tell you what spirits I see. There's a woman, indistinct, but definitely a woman. I sense sadness in her."

His eyes widened and he glanced about. "I never said I'd marry her." He waved one hand about his head, as though shooing away a mosquito. "Begone, pesky spirit. There was no need to throw yourself in the well. Stupid female." He rose and stomped away, with the last comment unclear whether he referred to the spirit or Jillian.

No tip. Lou had warned that men tipped when they were satisfied but lying made her a charlatan. Perhaps there was a way to spin her insight without deceit.

The next man hurried forward and planted himself in the booth. "My dear mother," he said as his Adam's apple bobbled up and down. "Did she suffer? Did she know my terrible sins before she passed?"

She eyed the fellow, a man in his fifties with a grizzled beard, a jagged, puckered scar at his hairline. "I see no spirits about you. Some souls advance right away and are content to wait in the next world."

He hung his head, forehead etched deep with creases. "I did dreadful things during the war. Horrible sins that haunt my dreams. I fear I will end up in a much darker place after death."

Her heart ached for the man, whichever side of the war he fought. People had been caught up in cataclysmic events they weren't able to control and made snap decisions under extreme stress. *We're all captives of our own eras.*

The best she could do was send the man away with a sense of peace. "Your mother must have known she'd see you again someday. Otherwise, wouldn't she have stayed and berated you from the grave?"

His head lifted, eyebrows raised in a hopeful expression. "Do you believe so?"

"Absolutely," she said, though she had no idea.

He sat in silence for a moment, and his lips trembled. Without a word, he dug a small gold nugget from his pocket and set it on the table. He gave her a brief nod, then left. The session left Jillian with a vague sense of guilt. If she stayed in this job long, she'd turn into a huckster-slash-counselor. Neither role appealed.

The night wore on and a small handful of gold nuggets and coins clinked in her pocket. She wasn't sure of the gold's value but appreciated each tip. Not every customer tipped, of course; just the ones satisfied with the outcome of their session. Although she knew the man with red suspenders didn't want to hear this truth—and that he wouldn't give her a tip if she told him—but innate honesty compelled her to inform him of his family's death, one after another of typhoid. His parents, two sisters, and an elderly aunt back in Missouri, all gone within days of each other, the aunt lingering in spirit in an effort to coax him home for the funerals. He dropped his head to the table and sobbed loudly, drawing stares from others in the room.

Lou sashayed across the room, her voluminous skirts sweeping aside those in her way. She laid a hand on the man's shoulder. "Lily is on the house for you tonight. No man leaves Lou's unhappy."

He wiped his eyes and stumbled to the waiting arms of Lily, who led him upstairs without a word.

Lou slid into the booth and faced Jillian with a scowl. "Did you hear what I said? No man leaves unsatisfied."

Above their heads the disembodied chuckle of a man's laugh echoed.

"The man's aunt wanted him to know about his family," she explained. "I felt it was a kindness to tell him, though I'm sure painful to hear."

"No stories about death and doom," Lou repeated. "Tell the men about fortune and loved ones who wait for them. Their sainted mothers who watch over them from heaven. That's what they desire and what gets the gold out of their pockets and into ours."

The chuckle grew louder and the faint outline of a man appeared.

"Lou, I see a spirit, a man, connected to you."

The madam laughed. "I don't doubt it. There have been plenty of men in my life."

"Gold-digging trollop," the spirit hissed, and settled in the booth beside Lou. Grossly corpulent, he appeared to be in his forties, with a golden beard shaped to a point. "I'll see you to your grave as you drove me to mine."

"Um, this one's not happy." Jillian twisted her lips in dismay.

The woman drew up her shoulders. "Think you're going to turn the tables on me, do you? I never disappointed a masher."

"Except her very own husband," the spirit growled.

"He claims to be your husband."

"Henry." Lou's voice came out in a harsh whisper.

She leaned forward on the table. "Prove he's here. Describe him."

"Large," Jillian said hastily, not wanting to use the word 'obese'. "Blond beard. He's wearing a black, striped suit with a white carnation in the top buttonhole."

"That's him," Lou said, sitting back, eyes wide. "Fat as a tick."

Henry chortled; his three chins waggled under the beard. "Tell her she's gotten old and wrinkled."

Choosing discretion, Jillian remained silent.

"So, the lily-livered deadbeat hangs around here, does he?" Lou sneered. "I thought I was well rid of him. What does he want?"

"What—" Jillian started, but the ghost broke in.

"I heard her," he snapped. "I may be dead but I'm not deaf. I have my reasons for staying nearby. I have property to safeguard."

"Property?" Jillian asked him. "What good are possessions? If you'd like a little advice, material belongings may be dragging you down."

A chilling howl rose from his throat, sending a man jumping to his feet then racing out the door. No one else appeared to notice.

"I didn't ask yer advice," the ghost said. "No need to mention property to Lou."

The madam's eyes narrowed; she regarded Jillian with sharp attention. "Where's the gold? Henry up and croaked, but not before he stashed half our gold. It's mine now, fair and square. Even in death, he's a no-good varmint."

His chuckle echoed around the booth. Henry appeared to enjoy his former wife's disgruntlement. His spirit clung to the woman with an iron grip.

"A lot of times ghosts don't remember their lives," Jillian said, thinking fast. "Their brains atrophy."

"I remember plenty," he retorted. "All the names she called me. The dish broken on my head that left a two-inch scar."

Lou's mouth sagged as she considered Jillian's words. "He always was pretty dumb."

"Yer the dim one. Right under your nose the past three years." His fleshy lips hovered next to Lou's ear. "Under the floor of yer favorite booth. Joke's on you."

Lou scratched her ear, the one he'd spoke into. Jillian considered her options. She had a wealth of knowledge...or knowledge of wealth.

Preparing herself for another howl from the cantankerous dead man, she murmured, "Lou, I have a business proposition for you."

The next ten minutes flew by in a rush of activity. She promised to inform the madam of the gold's location—for a price of ten dollars. Lou cleared the saloon, ordering everyone out into the street. Surprisingly, the men obeyed, although they grumbled and protested. Jillian stayed as the madam pried up the floorboards under the booth's table and retrieved four heavy bags. The woman cursed her husband as she fingered the gold.

Ten dollars wouldn't keep her safe for a month, let alone the remainder of Eva's pregnancy. But it would pay Catherine for the dresses, with a little left over.

This was a reminder that her gift could help people. No matter what the century, spirits wandered the Earth—some good, some bad. Either way, they had useful information for those they left behind.

Her shift completed and exhausted to her core, Jillian climbed stairs to the room on the third floor above the saloon Lou assigned to her. The prostitute who vacated the room three days earlier had left with a miner who promised to deed her a quarter share of his claim if she'd live with him a year and ease his loneliness. The room appeared to be a slight improvement on the Crocker mansion attic—the bed had a real mattress, and the rest of the furnishings consisted of a small wardrobe and mirror. And—lo and behold, a desk.

Inside one drawer lay several sheets of stiff paper and a dip pen and ink well. Her fingers itched to write her experiences over the past several days. Avid fans of Spirited Quest must wonder why she didn't update the blog.

If—*when*—she returned, she'd pen a thrilling story for her readers. Would anyone believe this wild tale?

Too tired to write, Jillian collapsed into bed. Tomorrow was a big day. In the morning, she'd seek out Lin, if it wasn't too late to save him from whatever plagued him.

Chapter Fifteen

Jillian woke to a heavy rain that thrummed against the window. Without a clock, she had no idea of the time, but the clip-clops of horses on the street below indicated the next day had arrived.

Lin.

His name drove her out of bed and into her clothes. She would find Eva's lover today. Tomorrow, Mason intended to exchange vows with someone else. She'd be damned if he would go to the altar with that sharp-clawed minx. If Lin either died or remained missing, Mason might have to stay in this era forever. Her stomach twinged at the idea of living as his mistress while he played house with Eva McAlister. Ugh. He was too damned chivalrous. Of course, his refusal to compromise his principles was one of the reasons she loved him.

With a borrowed umbrella in one hand and her wrapped uniform in the other, she set off through the sodden day in the direction of Sacramento's Chinatown, an area called *Yee Fow* by its inhabitants. The name meant "second city," she'd been told, with San Francisco known as *Daifow*, or "big city"—the two most important Chinese settlements in California.

Puddles abounded at the edges of the streets, and she took great care to avoid or leap over them. On some corners, boards had been laid across the flooded areas for pedestrians to keep their feet dry. In her mind, she pictured the dark river water creeping inch by inch upward, not constrained by levees. How much rain needed to fall before the city became a great inland lake? The slate gray sky showed no glimmer of sun and no intention of easing its steady rain.

Straight past downtown, left toward the river, and the streets changed. Chinese faces stared at her, a white woman who clearly didn't belong. To add to the disparity, most passersby were men. Jillian recalled her history, the laws against Chinese men shipping their wives to America, to discourage permanent settlement by the foreigners. Chinese men, too, didn't want to subject their wives to the dangers and western culture, and so kept their families back home. Still, some women made the voyage, as evident by those who peeked at her from doorways and behind windows.

She lifted her chin and strode forward with her umbrella held aloft. Mason's words returned to her: *When people step out of their roles, there are dire consequences.* But she had her laundry under her arm, a worker in need of a uniform cleaned. There could be no danger in that.

As she walked, she peered at storefronts for a particular tailor shop. Even in the rain, the area bustled with activity. Restaurants, general stores, hotels, and of course laundries and tailor shops. Even an opera house stood on one corner. Incense wafted from doorways, and a few shops featured ducks hanging in the windows.

The size of the area surprised her at first, but of course Sacramento served as the terminus of the intercontinental railroad and Chinese labor had been integral to its construction. She recalled a story from a long-ago history class where a railroad superintendent refused to hire the foreign workers. The man argued their slight stature meant they wouldn't be strong enough for the monumental task. Charles Crocker, who headed the Central Pacific Railroad, famously responded, "they built the Great Wall, didn't they?" And that was that.

Most store signs were lettered in Chinese and Jillian halted often to study windows for signs of a tailor shop.

Wisps of steam emanated from an open door. While she couldn't read the sign, the now-familiar odor of lye announced the business as a laundry. Inside, clothes hung on poles and a petite woman approached the counter to greet her.

Jillian folded her umbrella. "Good morning. I have a soiled uniform."

The woman bobbed her head and stretched out both hands to receive the package. "Tomorrow. You return."

"Yes, thank you. My name is Jillian Winchester."

The woman turned away with the package and disappeared into the steamy depth. Jillian hesitated to confirm their interaction had ended. She'd have to return the next day in hopes the uniform was ready. There hadn't even been an opportunity to ask about Lin.

Back on the boarded walkway, she again raised the umbrella. Muddy ruts had formed in the streets though people bustled along, darting covert glances her way.

A man in a fine three-piece suit and wide-brimmed hat stopped as she wavered about which direction to go next. "Are you lost?"

She heaved a sigh, grateful for the question. "I've been referred to a tailor shop, where a man named Lin works. I believe there are three brothers, including Lin, who own the business. Are you familiar with it?"

He bowed his head ever so slightly. "A fine establishment; they made this suit I wear now. Turn right at the next street. Halfway down." He sauntered on his way, an umbrella held high, as though soggy weather didn't bother him in the least.

With clear directions, Jillian hurried to the shop, a small storefront with Chinese lettering on the window. Inside, bolts of cloth stood upright, along with a series of hats, from workman style straw hats to a silk top hat. The shop clearly catered to a wide clientele.

A bell over the door jangled upon her entry. A tall, slender man in his mid-twenties, busy sweeping the floor, set aside his broom. He batted his hands against his sides as though to knock away dust. "Good day, ma'am." His words came out in the stilted accent of someone unaccustomed to speaking English. He turned his head and spoke in rapid Chinese to someone unseen in a back room.

Within seconds, a second man—this one a little older, and with slicked back hair—emerged and stepped in front of the other man. "Yes. How may we help you?" His English flowed easier, the accent less pronounced.

She took a deep breath. The aroma of sandalwood wafted through the orderly room. Now that she was here, her mission seemed daunting. "I-I'd like to speak with Lin. I understand he works here, in this business."

His face stayed blank, but a wariness entered his eyes. "I am his brother, Jiang, and this is Zhen." The younger man gave a short bow of his head. "Lin has left for other ventures. But I would be pleased to help you."

"It's Lin I need to see. Could you tell me where I can find him?" She cast her glance around the pristine shop, filled with bolts of gray and black cloth. Tweeds, wools, cotton, and even silk. A small case with bow ties stood in the corner and more hats hung on the wall.

Lin, are you here? she asked in her mind.

"I am sorry, but as I said, he no longer works in the shop." Jiang's words remained polite, but frostiness had entered his tone.

The patter of rain against the window filled the silence as she sought a reason to prompt Lin's whereabouts. The truth might serve her purpose; if she spoke Eva's name, Lin might appear. "There is a young woman of my acquaintance who seeks him. Her brother visited this shop a week ago on her behalf. Evaline McAlister."

The brothers exchanged glances and the younger muttered low in Chinese.

"I can tell you know what I'm talking about," she said. "This is important not just to her, but to me as well. It's imperative I see your brother today." She peered around the room. *Lin, hurry, speak to me.*

Zhen marched to the front of the store and paced by the door, as though too agitated to stay still. "The rich white woman does not understand our customs," Jiang said. "She preyed on Lin's innocence."

Jillian stared at the older brother. "They are both young and innocent. They fell in love. They want to be together." It was *essential* they were united for Mason to be freed from Eva's clutches. "I need to speak with Lin, for my own reasons as well."

A click behind her made her whirl. Zhen stood in the doorway, a key in his hand.

"What are you doing?" she gasped.

"Zhen," Jiang said, his voice stern. "Do you want to bring the sheriff to our door?"

Zhen remained in place with legs apart. "She will cause trouble. We must keep her here until Lin is on the ship." He then switched to rapid-fire Chinese, his tone sharp while his brother's face grew red.

Jiang banged a hand on the counter and responded in English. "Unlock the door. We cannot kidnap a white woman. You will get us hanged."

"She has no right to make demands on us. She does not belong."

"Zhen!" Jiang's voice sharpened. "We Chinese are not allowed to testify in court. If the sheriff comes, her word alone will convict us. Unlock the door."

The younger brother's anger and hatred rippled over her—not for herself, but for what she represented: the prejudice, restrictions, and unfairness of his adopted country. Would anyone on the street help her if she screamed?

He unlocked the door with a snap. His expression indicated he believed that was the wrong decision.

"Where is Lin going?" Jillian demanded. "Which ship?"

"This is not a good place for our brother," Jiang said, arms crossed over his puffed up chest. "If he stays, he will bring shame upon our parents. We have written of this problem to our father. Our parents have chosen a proper wife for him back home in Guangdong. Lin will leave next week."

"Doesn't your brother have the right to choose his

own wife, and his own future?"

"You Americans believe everyone should live for themselves, never a thought for anyone else, never having family honor," Jiang said in an even tone. "After Lin is married, perhaps with a son or two, he can return." His voice grew softer. "Surely you can understand, there is no future for him with a white woman. Already, we fear for his life."

Choosing her words with care, Jillian firmed her shoulders. "And what if he has a son here?"

Zhen's eyebrows lowered; he took a menacing step forward. "The white concubine? She is nothing."

The older brother blinked rapidly but didn't speak. A shadow shifted out of a corner and glided forward.

"I must see Eva," the shadow said, taking on Lin's shape. "Tell her I will refuse to marry anyone else."

Jillian faced Lin's spirit; relief flooded her that he appeared. Her instinct had been right. He remained in Chinatown. "She is also in trouble." She glanced at his brothers, who gaped at her. "Eva carries your child and must marry someone soon, or she fears her father will cast her out of the house. She…" the words stuck in her throat, "she plans to marry Mason tomorrow."

"*Wu—sorcer*ess." Zhen breathed the word and joined his brother by the counter.

The shadow took full shape, tall and lean, and the anguish evident on his face. "My brothers keep me in the cellar, sedated on opium. Do not let her marry another man. The key is on a hook by the register."

The realization struck Jillian why the spirit appeared so dark and strange. Lin wandered a world between life and death, through a murky haze of opium. She addressed the other men. "Your brother wants to marry Eva, regardless of the consequences. He deserves to make his own decision."

The two men eyed her warily. The older brother spoke. "If the woman carries his child, that is her fate. Our brother has a different *mìngyùn,* another destiny."

Zhen clutched at his brother's arm. "Send her away. She is cursed."

Jillian was tempted to play on his fears and threaten to cast a spell if they didn't release Lin. Instead, she gave a quick nod to the spirit and backed toward the door. The situation remained too volatile, and no way to overcome the two brothers alone. She needed help.

"I see I've made a mistake." Under their glare, she fumbled for the doorknob, breath high in her throat. Out in the street, she lifted her skirts to her ankles to hasten away from the tailor shop. After a couple glances over her shoulder assured her the brothers weren't in pursuit, her pace slowed.

Two streets farther, she stopped to lean against a storefront. The wide eaves gave her cover from the rain that had slowed to a drizzle. Black clouds hung over the city. In her rush, she'd left the umbrella behind and water dripped down her neck. Instead of being cool, the day had turned humid and sticky. A carriage rumbled by, followed by a mule cart. Each splashed through standing water on the muddy road. She picked up her skirts again, this time to prevent them from dragging in the mud and water and headed toward the forge.

****

Jillian stepped to the top of her ankles in a puddle. Small pools of water gathered everywhere. Her new dress, which needed to suffice for the next few days, was a mess. Most streets were now empty of people; only the occasional mule cart passed by. The low rumble of thunder warned her that more rain threatened. No wonder city streets were raised; otherwise, they would soon be underwater.

Somewhere in the distance a church bell tolled, its deep, even tones somber. An appropriate, dismal day for a funeral. She sloshed her way to the blacksmith, and her heart raced with the news she had to share with Mason. The next challenge would be his, in effecting Lin's escape.

The fire in the forge burned low, and tools hung in their proper place. A boy, perhaps ten years old, stacked crates in a corner. Jillian ventured inside the door. "Is Mason around? I need to see him."

The lad grunted as he shoved a crate into place before giving her a once-over look. "He's at the tailor shop—he's getting married in the morning, lucky dog."

She clenched her hands into fists. "I'm well aware of his impending wedding. I have important news for him about those nuptials. *Very* important news."

The boy winked. "I'll bet. I've heard about you and the blacksmith. Word's around that you're his kiss n' cuddle. With a room at Lou's, too."

How in the world had the boy learned so much? Of course, why would she assume her movements unnoticed? "Just tell me where I'll find him," she said through gritted teeth.

The boy leaned against the wall. "How much do you earn at Lou's? I bet a bundle."

She dug in her pocket and retrieved a quarter. The coin displayed Lady Liberty seated and brandishing a flag. "Here. Now talk."

He snatched the coin from her hand and thrust it in a pocket. "Well, look who it is." He nodded toward the door and dashed away.

Mason strode in, his expression alight when he saw her. "Jillian. I checked at Lou's, but you weren't there. Where have you been?"

The boy had lied, nasty beast. Her relief that Mason was here replaced her annoyance at the kid and his extortion.

Mason crossed quickly to her and grasped her hand, his forehead furrowed. "How was the night at Lou's? I hope none of the men got out of line."

"Lou keeps them in check. She's a wonder." Jillian squeezed his hand. "I have important news. I've found Lin."

Mason stepped back and eyed her. "You don't waste time. Tell me."

"His brothers have him held captive. They've drugged him and plan to ship him to China." She recounted the confrontation with the two brothers, and Lin's appearance. "Am I right to suspect the sheriff wouldn't get involved?"

"The situation might become worse for Lin if the sheriff discovered his affair with a white woman." He folded muscled arms against his broad chest. "I'll get him out of there."

"And then send him on his way with Eva." Jealousy surged in her again. "Before the wedding."

He caught her up in his arms. "Then we go home."

"Sounds easy enough," Jillian said.

Mason snorted. "It's always a bit of an adventure with you, isn't it?"

She sighed and backed away. "I didn't ask for any

of this. When we get back, I intend to be the biggest homebody you've ever seen. Gardening and home improvement projects. Maybe I'll start a cooking blog."

The boy trotted in, a chortle in his throat as he glanced between the two of them. "Hey boss. Filled the water troughs, cleaned the stalls. Need me to stand guard outside for a few minutes, make sure of your privacy?"

Mason acted fast; one arm whipped out and grasped the boy by the neck. "Don't be bloody cheeky."

The kid writhed and wrenched free. "What'd you do that for? I wanna help."

Mason gave the boy an assessing gaze. "If that's the case, Thomas, I have a job for you." He glanced at Jillian, then back. "Hitch Sally to the old cart and wait around the side for me. We're going on an errand."

Thomas' face lit up. "Both of us? You and me?"

"Mason, you don't even have a plan." Now with a rescue operation in motion, Jillian's stomach clenched.

He grinned at her, a lazy quirk of his lips. The lines at the corners of his eyes creased into his weathered face. "Planning's just another way to do nothing," he quipped. "Go on now, lad."

Thomas darted toward the stables. Once the boy traveled out of earshot, Mason strode to a chest by one wall. He dug a key out of a pocket, unlocked it, and removed a holster and pistol. Her heart skipped a beat and then raced forward.

"You don't know how to use a pistol," she said, her voice faint.

He checked the cylinders, loaded two more bullets, then clicked it closed with an expert flick of his hand. His hazel eyes flickered with a memory. "Well enough to get the business done." The heavy stamp of a mule's hooves sounded through the wall. He strapped the holster around his hips. "Listen, we need to free Lin right away and get him and Eva out of town. Your task is to tell her to pack a bag and get supplies ready."

She swallowed hard. This was moving too fast. Those were real bullets he loaded in the gun. "Don't...don't take the pistol."

He gripped her by the shoulders. "Don't falter now. This is our chance—Lin and Eva, you and me. You feel certain we can get back to our own time?"

Doubt suffused her, racing through her veins. The heat of the forge, the danger Mason now faced, made her dizzy. She was sure of nothing. But they had to try. It wouldn't do to sap his confidence now.

She steadied her voice to camouflage the lie. "Yes, I'm sure."

Chapter Sixteen

Wind whipped at Jillian's skirts, and tangled them around her legs. She kicked at the heavy folds of material that constrained her stride. After half a mile toward Eva's house, she took shelter in a doorway from the warm rain. A riot of scents swirled with each damp gust—of livestock, mud, pastureland, damp wood, and cigar smoke.

Voices from inside a store carried to her. "The river is rising fast. Already, the south has become swampland. People have moved to the ridge."

"We're safe enough here, I hope, now that the streets are raised."

Jillian glanced around. To her knowledge, Sacramento's terrain lay flat, at least fifteen miles away from the foothills with no rises. If the city flooded, her safest recourse was her third-floor room at Lou's. But her immediate task took her in the opposite direction from Lou's, to warn Eva to gather supplies and be ready to flee. The pampered young woman was unprepared for the rough life ahead. The young couple needed to outrun Eva's father, who would be sure to launch a pursuit. Lin's brothers, too, would set out after them. Even if they evaded discovery, each day forward promised difficulties as a mixed-race couple.

Was love worth this much effort? Instantly, she realized the irrationality of her doubt. Hadn't she decided to stay in the past for Mason if all else failed, to put up with his marriage to another woman, to work in a saloon as a clairvoyant? Whomever said love drove people to extremes wasn't kidding.

She stepped out from the doorway just as a carriage jolted to a stop next to her and the door swung open. Eva's face appeared from inside, mouth pursed in disapproval. "For heaven's sake. Get in."

Without hesitation, Jillian clambered inside and sat with a thud on the padded seat. Water dripped down her nose and she swiped it away. With her new dress soaked, the corset gripped her middle tighter than ever.

Eva wrinkled her nose. "Must you always appear so disheveled?" Pink ribbons hung from her hair, done up in intricate ringlets. An afternoon gown in matching blush rose high on her throat, its collar adorned with a delicate lace pattern.

"Sorry, I left my carriage in the twenty-first century," Jillian snapped. "And by the way, we don't have horses and carriages then."

Eva rolled her eyes. "What news do you have for me?"

To think Mason risked his life for this twit. But the four of them were bound together for now. "I found him, or at least I know where he is."

The young woman gasped and leaned forward. "Where? Take me to him!"

"His brothers have kept him drugged and captive. Their intent is to send him back to China to marry a suitable woman there."

"Suitable! My father is an important man."

Ignoring the outburst, Jillian summed up the conversation with the brothers and Lin's brief appearance. "Mason is on his way there now to free him, at great personal risk." Tears sprang to her eyes at the memory of the pistol in his hands. A glance at Eva showed the young woman impassive at the idea of Mason in danger. Her tone hardened. "You need to be ready to leave, with whatever supplies you can gather. Tonight. *Before* the wedding."

"Lin would never marry another woman. He loves *me*." Eva leaned back, a hard glint in her eyes. The fact *she* meant to marry Mason in the next twenty-four hours apparently didn't cross her mind. She thumped on the roof and a moment later the driver opened the door. "Miss?"

"I've changed my mind. I'll visit my friend Eleanor tomorrow." She gestured toward Jillian. "This unfortunate woman needs to go to McCreary's general store. She's in need of…boots…an umbrella…and other items."

The driver hesitated. Water streamed off his wide-brimmed hat. "The rain has increased. Your father wouldn't like you out in this weather. I'm sure he'd be worried. And the horse—"

Eva waved a regal hand. "Then we'd better be quick about it, shouldn't we?" The door closed and the carriage rumbled forward. Eva bit her lip. "Do you have any money? Father doesn't give me—"

"Right," Jillian interrupted, and dug into her skirt pocket for the proceeds of the previous evening. "How you and Lin are going to survive on your own is beyond me." She dropped five dollars and two gold nuggets into Eva's hand. "You'll need to get a job, be useful." She swallowed back fear of what danger Mason could be facing at that very moment; she needed to focus on her own task.

As the carriage jolted to a halt outside the store, the rain let up long enough for them to hasten in. A roll of thunder grew until the windows shook, followed by a torrent of rain.

"You ladies shouldn't be out in this, and your horse and driver either," the proprietor said. "Your errand can't be this important."

Eva glanced at Jillian, as though unsure how to handle the situation. The woman was useless, even in the middle of civilization.

"You'll do us a favor by being quick," Jillian said. "To start with, we need some blankets, dried beans, and flour."

They hurried about the store, gathered up items and piled them on the counter in a growing heap. Within a few minutes, the grocer had tallied the lot—fifteen dollars. Eva placed the gold nuggets along with the five dollars in coins before the man.

He shook his head with a frown. "That'd be eight dollars, tops."

The young woman raised her eyebrows at Jillian. "There's not enough here."

"Then you'll need to put some items back."

Eva's bottom lip pooched out at the words, but she sorted through the goods and removed a frying pan and a sack of cornmeal. Jillian elbowed past her, shoved away a pair of silk stockings, two feather pillows, a lace parasol, and a bolt of lavender calico and grabbed back the pan and cornmeal. The grocer nodded and wrapped their packages in brown paper.

Their coachman, whose face looked as stormy as the sky, helped them ferry the goods inside the carriage.

"We'll stash all this at your father's stables, in one of the empty stalls," Jillian said. "Then you will go home as usual and wait to hear from one of us."

Eva's wide eyes shone. "I can't wait to see my love again. It's been so long."

"Let's get a move on. Before your driver and horse drown."

****

Supplies stashed in a horse stall at the livery, Eva and the carriage departed. Jillian sank to rest on a hay bale. What delayed Mason and Thomas? What if Mason didn't return at all? She rose and paced down the length of the stables.

A horse nickered softly, and its head emerged above the stall door. She stroked the animal's long face and patted its chocolate brown neck. "We're both in need of a little comfort right now."

How long had it been? Two hours at least. Her gaze traveled repeatedly to the stable doors. The rain had softened to a harmless sprinkle, causing a million little ripples in the standing water. The horse nudged her shoulder with its nose, and she smiled despite her worry. Animals had spirits too; she had spoken with a few on a trip to the Yukon where she sought the spirit animals that guided and protected the peoples of the far north for centuries. Their voices were like the gentle nudge of this horse—not a literal voice, but a suggestion that often needed no interpretation.

The dull trot of a mule broke into her musings, sending her racing for the door. Thomas held the reins, alone. Her heart leaped and she swung both stable doors wide to enable the cart entry. "Where's Mason?" she cried as soon as the cart entered.

Thomas wagged his chin toward the cart. "In the back, with the Chinaman. I rescued them both."

Mason's voice rose from the cart. "Here." He threw off a large tarp. A bloody gash showed in his pant leg. Lin lay next to him, eyes closed and still as death.

"You've been hurt!" She hoisted herself onto the cart to crouch next to him. "His brothers attacked you?"

"Not the brothers. They were easy enough to subdue. I held the pistol on them while Thomas tied them up." Mason gestured toward Lin's motionless body. "This one stabbed me with my own knife. He fought me and grabbed it when I tried to lift him. There's gratitude for you."

Lin's inert body rested on the cart's boards, his face familiar from the Crocker mansion. Had they rescued a man who didn't want to be free? "Why did he fight you?"

"He lay just like this, in an opium daze, when I first picked him up. I don't believe he understood what he was doing, but it hurts all the same." Mason probed below the slashed fabric at his leg and winced.

"You can tell me the details later. Let's get your leg taken care of first."

While Thomas unhitched the mule, then led it into a dry stall, she washed and dressed Mason's wound as best she could. Once more, the concern over the lack of antibiotics niggled at the back of her mind. The gash stretched long but wasn't very deep and might not require stitches. All the while, Lin slept on. His black lashes lay against high cheekbones and his lips full and slightly parted. His chest rose and fell rhythmically.

"How long do you think before he comes to?"

Mason shook his head. "They must have let him

rouse from time to time to eat and drink. Otherwise, he'd be dead by now. His brothers must have kept him in this state for weeks, ever since they discovered his affair with Eva." He rummaged under the tarp and withdrew a small leather pouch. "I found some opium in the cellar, in case he needs to withdraw over time. Otherwise, the lure to return may be too great. Let's hope his will is strong."

"And Eva's as well," Jillian said. "She's in for a rude awakening away from her father's protection and money. We bought blankets and other supplies today. In the stall over there."

He tested his leg, and gingerly rose to inspect the goods with a slight limp. One more strike against Lin and Eva in her estimation. She narrowed her eyes and glared at the prone figure. She had a few choice words to say to the man when he woke up.

****

Hours later, his brown eyes blinked open and stared into hers. "I thought you were a dream."

"You." Jillian's voice trembled. "You stole us from our own time."

"I do not understand." Lin struggled to prop himself up to look around the stable. "Where am I? How did I get here?"

Mason came up behind her. "Jillian, be gentle. He's been drugged."

She whirled on him. "We don't have time to go slow. He needs to leave town tonight."

"My brothers…" Lin's eyes widened as though in memory. "They fed me opium, kept me in the cellar…"

She gripped her skirts to keep herself from shaking the man. "Yes, and Mason rescued you. In gratitude,

169

you *stabbed* him."

He rubbed his forehead. "I-I wounded him? I do not recall."

"The main thing is you are free, and can make your own decision about your future," Mason said in a stern tone. "The question is about Eva. Do you want to be with her, marry her? She carries your child."

Lin scrambled to his feet and immediately stumbled to his knees. "Eva! Where is she?"

Mason laid a hand on his shoulder. "Home safe, waiting until dark so you both can leave town. For now, you need to rest and detox a bit."

Lin sat back on the stall floor and shook his head. "What is this detox you say?"

"Let the opium leave your system. You'll need your wits about you. Your lives will depend on it."

Jillian handed Lin a cup of water and settled on a hay bale to observe this person who so drastically changed her life and controlled her future. The man sipped the water until he drained the cup. "You said you remembered me. Do you recall how you reached out to me, how you brought me to you?"

Lines furrowed his forehead. "In my dream," he spoke haltingly, "you glowed in a golden light and drifted among all worlds. Everything hid in a thick fog, but not you."

Her breath quickened. Never before had a spirit explained how they found her from their other dimension. "What else did you see?"

"It was clear to me the woman in my dream would lead me out of my dilemma, if I could touch her. But she…you…appeared so far away, as though in a distant land." His gaze shifted to Mason. "Then you were before me, and with a connection with this woman."

"So you grabbed him to get at me," Jillian interrupted.

Lin's attention returned to her. An awareness flashed in his eyes before he closed them. He knew more than he admitted. "I had to. There was no other way." He peered around once more. "This was a dream though, not reality. But here you both are."

One detail still nagged at her mind. His story didn't add up. "Mason arrived here three years ago, long before you even met Eva, or had your dream. How did you arrange for him to meet her?" In truth, a thousand more questions crowded her mind, but Lin's eyelids drooped and he would sleep again soon.

He shrugged and leaned against the stall. His voice grew softer. "Time and place meant nothing in my dream. I set him in Eva's brother's path, as easy as if he were a piece on a checkerboard, to keep him nearby. He became more useful than expected. In my dream, I watched him and waited for you. Our fates were meant to intersect and help one another."

"We wouldn't have needed help if you didn't drag us here."

She sounded peevish, but kinder words refused to come. Her new prickly self, the one that had emerged here in this era, dominated. Mason might have been killed in his attempt to rescue Lin and the possibility remained they could be trapped here. If they couldn't leave, repercussions might follow for their role in Eva and Lin's disappearance. The story about a rash elopement would fall apart. She and Mason needed to flee Sacramento one way or another.

Mason laid a hand on her arm. "We need to let Lin

rest and recover. He has a long journey tonight and many nights to come. Give him a few hours of sleep and then we can talk some more."

"One more question first. How could you do this to us? Such a selfish act. You've monkeyed around with our lives." Fury drove her words. She bit back more accusations. They needed Lin's help and goodwill.

Lin scooted into a bedding of straw. "We are all pieces in a puzzle." Almost instantly his face and limbs relaxed as he fell into a deep slumber.

With a frustrated snort, Jillian rose and joined Mason at the far end of the stables. She positioned herself with a clear view of where Lin slept. He was the key to their return, and she loathed to let him out of sight. The Chinese man had a unique gift, with the ability to travel through time and organize people's lives.

"I don't believe all he says," she said in a hushed voice. "There's more to this. In any case, we have to leave before they do. Once Lin is gone, our capability to go home may disappear."

Mason scratched his beard. "And if Lin believes we are integral to his freedom, he may want us around longer. Even past the time they have left the city."

Lin could keep them in this era indefinitely, scurrying at his beck and call—a sort of time-travel blackmail. He was now free, but they remained his captive.

Disquiet flickered in her mind. "Then we'll be stuck here forever."

Chapter Seventeen

Thomas sauntered into the stable, his arms laden with a small crate. "Hi-ho, the hero returns." He halted before the stall where Lin slept and gave a snort. "Still in a stupor? Opium's not for me. I'd rather have a fishing pole or a double helping of blueberry pie."

Mason strode forward and took the crate from the boy's arms. "Good lad. Stay clear of drugs."

Thomas shoved his hands in his pockets and nodded toward the box. "Speaking of which, there's two bottles of laudanum there, all my friend had on hand. Not easy since he pilfers from the apothecary where he works. I owe him a big favor now." He faced Mason. "Which means you owe me. Sandwiches and strawberries for you and the lady are in there, and the Chinaman if he ever wakes up. I got the soap and gauze you asked for, too."

Jillian rose from her own stall, their voices wakening her from a nap. There promised to be a long night ahead for all of them. She dusted straw off her skirts, still damp from the rain, and joined them. Thomas smirked at her.

"Laudanum," she observed. "Isn't that a pain medicine made from opium?"

Mason handed her a sandwich and unwrapped one of his own. "Lin may need it to wean himself off the pure substance. They need to be far away from the city

before he runs out, so he's not tempted to turn back."
He clapped a hand on Thomas' shoulder. "I'll get you a
fishing pole down at McCreary's—maybe even some
blueberry pie. You've done a good day's work."

Thomas thrust out his chest, his eyes alight.
"You'd have been in a heap of trouble without me
today. What'd you want with that fellow, anyway?"

"Best not to say for now," Mason said, with a
glance at Jillian. "It'll come out soon enough, I fear.
But remember what I said."

The boy's forehead creased. "You said you're off
to elope with the boss' daughter, when you could be
king of the castle when he dies. It doesn't make sense.
You have her father's permission and a dandy wedding
set. There will be a fine feast prepared—and all the
cake you can eat."

Mason took a bite of the sandwich. "I feel the need
for a change of scenery."

"Did you steal the Chinaman to be your slave?"
Thomas shook his head, his forehead scrunched. "I
don't like the foreigners, but slavery is a sin."

Jillian selected two massive strawberries from the
box, the sweet aroma almost ambrosial. "Mason simply
wants to free the man from his captivity, an act of
goodness. Nothing more than that. After tonight, Lin
will be gone too."

"Lin. They sure have funny names."

"I bet they'd find Thomas a strange name in
China," Jillian said. She bit into the plump strawberry
and juice flooded her mouth. These were berries at peak
season, fresh from the fields.

A groan arose from Lin as he stirred.

"Off with you now." Mason waved a hand at

Thomas and spoke hurriedly. "I need the forge swept and the fire stoked. Keep an eye out for customers. They'll be back now that the rain has stopped."

Thomas eyed Lin's limp form. "You want to be rid of me. There weren't any secrets or intrigue before this one arrived." He glared pointedly at Jillian. "Is she to go with you as well, in your elopement?"

"Never you mind. The less you see and hear today, the better." Mason gestured to the door. "Go."

The boy traipsed away, calling over his shoulder, "Don't forget my fishing pole before you leave. You promised."

Lin groaned again and struggled to sit up. "Where am I? What have you done to me?"

Jillian and Mason rushed to his side. "You are safe," Mason said, "and out of your brothers' control."

"My stomach, my legs. Oh, my head. I think I will be sick."

Jillian knelt next to him and unwrapped the sandwich in her hand. "It's the opium leaving your system. You need to eat and drink."

Lin shoved the food away and clutched his stomach. "I cannot eat." His eyes wild as his gaze searched his surroundings. "Please help me, my body is in anguish."

Mason withdrew to the back of the stable where the cart stood. He strode back, in his hands a syringe and a small pouch. "Your pain is little more than a desire for opium. How much did your brothers give you?"

Lin's focus steadied on the syringe. "Dissolve three pinches in water. Large pinches."

"That kept you unconscious through the day. You've become reliant, so we must get you off this drug if you want to be with Eva."

Lin fell back. "Eva." His tone was soft, tormented.

Mason stirred two pinches of opium into a small amount of water then drew the cloudy liquid into the syringe. "We'll try a lower dose. You must be strong or the drug will be your jailor, not your brothers."

"Yes, but be quick." He unbuttoned his sleeve and exposed the inside of his arm. A rainbow of bruises, some faded and others bright, marred his skin.

Jillian winced and turned away as Mason injected the opium. She strolled to the stable door. Weak sunshine strove to break through the clouds, which had ceased their showers, at least for the moment. The everyday noise of a city at work resumed: the steady clip-clop of horses, the chink of metal on brick. A door slammed and voices rumbled. The air smelled fresh as though the rain washed the city clean. The storm had given them cover during their flurry of afternoon activity, but how soon until Lin's brothers sought out their former captive?

A soft shuffle drew her attention back to the men. "Ah, much better," Lin sighed, as he propped himself up. A dreamy look suffused his eyes.

"You must eat some food." Mason pressed a sandwich into the other man's hands. Lin complied in listless obedience.

"Eva won't be up to this." Jillian rejoined them. There was nothing to do but speak the uncomfortable truth. These star-crossed lovers wouldn't last a week. "Deal with an opium addict? Sleep on the ground? I doubt she even knows how to cook."

"I know how to cook," Lin said, laying the sandwich on his lap. His speech was slow and ever-so-slightly slurred. "Eva is stronger than you give her credit for. She is a tiger, strong and confident and stubborn. She will not be defeated by difficulties. I am a horse, a helper, and the tiger is my perfect match. Together, we will overcome all obstacles."

"If that is the case, then Mason and I are free to leave."

Lin renewed chewing on the sandwich, then took a long drink of water. He gave her a steady stare. "Do not be in such a hurry. When Eva and I leave the city, there will be nothing to stop your own travels. Until then, consider how remarkable your journey has been. You have done what others can only dream of doing."

Mason refilled the water cup and set it at Lin's elbow. "Have you done this before—kidnapped someone from another time?"

Jillian leaned forward. Who was this man—the spirit—able to transport people from another time to do his bidding?

"Once," he mused. "I was twelve, still in China. The man spoke a different dialect, so I did not understand most of what he said. He could not understand me either and ran off. I felt terrible he did not wait so I might help him return to his own time." Lin shrugged in an offhand manner and finished his sandwich. "My grandfather had this secret gift, as did his grandfather."

She stared at him. "You've never facilitated a return?"

"Oh, I suppose there was one other time." He chuckled, a self-deprecatory sound. "A woman, very beautiful, who I wanted very much to meet. I was seventeen and idealistic. I believed if I loved her, she would love me back." He lifted his chin. "When I refused to let her go, she threatened to kill me and then herself. I realized she would never love me. I believe she made it home safely."

This selfish and infuriating man! A perfect match for Eva. She fought down her irritation. "Sounds as though you've distressed everyone you've taken, for your own use. You must give your word you won't kidnap anyone else. And that you won't abduct us again, even if you and Eva run into trouble."

His eyelids drooped and he lay back on the straw. "Once Eva and I leave the city limits, our connection will be broken. Your era will call to you through the passageway through which you arrived. Go there and your fate will ensue, one way or another." He closed his eyes. "As to the other…I cannot promise our paths will not cross again."

Mason tapped her arm and they retreated to let Lin sleep. The big animals shifted in their stalls, heads lifting with interest as they passed. "You can't do any more here. You should return to Lou's, and I need to work. We both need to act normal and be ready for tonight. Once Eva's household is asleep, I'll launch them on their way."

Weak rays of late afternoon sunshine flickered through the clouds and lit the stable window. She swallowed hard. They had hours to wait and so much could go wrong in that time. "They'll still be in danger from Eva's father."

"Thomas will spread the story we eloped, and that fearing her family's anger, we decided to create a life for ourselves back East. That will mask the true story. And if he sends a search party, they won't be expecting her in the company of a Chinese man."

"Lin's brothers will know."

"They may be fearful that because they attacked me, they could be thrown in prison. The law would treat them with harsh justice. I don't think they'll launch a search right away, and that may give Lin and Eva enough time to get away."

For the first time, she was hopeful of success. "I'll be back at midnight."

****

Two pairs of dancers swayed to the jangling tunes at Lou's saloon. Unlike the quick pace of the piano, their movements were languid, more a pre-coupling than a dance. First one, then the other twosome disappeared up the staircase to the ever-busy second-floor business.

At her corner booth, despite her distraction by the wall clock's endlessly slow movement toward midnight, Jillian tried to focus on the man sitting opposite her. "I don't see a spirit with you tonight," she said. "Sometimes, that's the case."

The man's knuckles grew white as he clenched his fists on the polished-wood table. "The last guy got a spirit—he said so. A pretty gal he courted back home."

She sighed. Many of the men who sat at her table yearned for someone lost, many times a sweetheart or mother who had succumbed to sickness or an accident. "Not everyone gets a spirit of their own. Count yourself lucky. They're not all content. They *are* dead, you know."

He lit a cigar; the heavy-scented smoke joined a similar cloud of haze that drifted above. "Probe a little harder. A whore up at the camps liked me a whole lot.

Little gal, a bit peaked looking. She's likely dead and I bet her ghost is lonely."

This was doubtful, but Jillian humored him another minute and then shook her head. "No, I'm sorry. There's no one here for you."

He scooted to the edge of the booth. "Well, the fellers at the bar are expectin' I have someone, so I'll just say the whore showed up. Don't go disputing me."

"Deal."

He slid a coin across the table, and she pocketed it before another glance at the clock. The hour hand edged past eleven. Another patron and she would be done. She arranged her skirts and tucked a loose strand of hair into place.

The next customer's presence loomed over the table. Heat crept up her neck. The Crockers' gardener glared down at her. "Zeb! I, uh, what a surprise."

He slid into the booth. "I heard you worked here, but I didn't believe it. I never did understand women and their natural inclination toward sin."

She fought not to roll her eyes. "I guess that's why you're here, too."

His forehead furrowed. "That's different. I'm a man. And I don't frequent this place."

"If it'll make you feel better, my entire job is right here in this booth. Not upstairs."

Across the smoky saloon, Lou surveyed her realm from her usual booth. A well-dressed man clad in a dark suit and vest sat next to her, a hand high up on her thigh. A couple traipsed down the stairs, the fellow hiking at his pants. The woman, an emerald feather in her hair that danced with every step, approached another potential customer at the bar.

Zeb took in the scene with a frown. "I reckon you're clad like a modest woman. Not like the others here." He cleared his throat. "But you prey on men just the same. You take their money and pretend to be something you're not, as you did at the Crockers'."

A hint of a threat seeped into his tone and she stiffened. "I don't know what you mean."

"They have the sheriff on the lookout for you. Lying like you did to gain entry to the house. Mrs. Crocker never gave you a job. She never saved you from the streets. It all spilled out after you left."

Her glance flew to the door. "The sheriff?"

"At least the whores do an honest trade. A man knows what he's paid for." His upper lip curled. "With you, it's all lies and plain robbery, deceiving innocent citizens." He snorted. "If there's any type of ghost you conjure here, it's evil spirits."

Beneath the table, her hands twisted in her skirts. Was the sheriff on his way? "You won't have to worry. I don't plan to stay long."

With a sneer on his face, he slid from the booth. "The wages of sin are death."

"Zeb, wait." Her heart thudded against her chest. He halted, his face turned away. "Is the sheriff coming for me tonight? Give me tonight and I'll be gone. I promise."

His jaw tightened and a muscle showed in his cheek. The emerald-feathered prostitute at the bar led her next client to the staircase. Zeb's gaze followed them up the steps. When they reached the second floor, he gave a sharp nod. "I won't say a word until after the sun comes up." He thrust the saloon door open and it banged closed behind him.

She didn't hesitate. The Crocker house would be on alert now her deception had been uncovered and she branded a charlatan. Entry certain to be more difficult than she anticipated. But there was no other option.

Chapter Eighteen

Jillian fought back the temptation to say goodbye to Lou and thank the madam for giving her a job and place to stay. The fewer people who knew her plans, the better. If Zeb didn't keep his word, or if events went awry, every minute of subterfuge mattered. Let the sheriff search the premises or wait in her room for her return. Maybe the Crockers' gardener spoke the truth—she was not an honest woman, at least not in this century.

She left through the saloon kitchen. Smoke from the stove hovered above her head and drifted out the open door into a dark alley. The stench of garbage moldered in the damp. A cat yowled and a small unseen creature splashed through a puddle. Hair prickled on the back of her neck. Before she had time to reconsider, she forged ahead, and a moment later hurried out of the alley into a wide street.

She didn't bother to return to her third-story room. There was nothing important there. Coins and a couple of gold nuggets jangled in her pocket, including one marble-sized nugget she'd saved. The next few hours would determine whether she and Mason returned to their century or ended up on the run like Lin and Eva.

The picture in the mansion flickered into her mind. Goodness and vice on the same canvas, with the message within proclaiming each person possessed both traits and able to choose which way to go. This era had brought out the worst in her: a prickly side to her nature, impatience, and—for the first time—mistrust of a spirit who asked her assistance. The bald truth was she would have left Lin in the cellar and a pregnant Eva to her own fate. But there was no other way home.

How hard her heart had grown. If she stayed in this century, what other character flaws might she discover? In contrast, the stress of this journey had made Mason a better man. Kind, steady, thoughtful. He already possessed these traits, but his goodness had grown more dominant.

Cool darkness enveloped her as she strode toward the stable. No urban city lights aided her vision. Twice she stumbled. Music, laughter, and the rumble of voices emanated from saloon doors. Despite the hour, a handful of people lingered about, all men, who gave her curious glances. "Respectable" women didn't roam the streets near midnight. She kept her chin down and tried not to act like a frightened rabbit. Every noise tensed her shoulders and she wished she had a canister of pepper spray.

She still didn't have a plan how to obtain access to the Crocker mansion in the middle of the night. The doors would be locked, and the household likely roused if she broke a window. Mason had risked his life to rescue Lin; he relied on her to get them inside the house. She fingered the coins and gold in her pocket. Perhaps a bribe to one of the live-in servants would accomplish the task. One more transgression to add to her tally.

A brown rat scuttled out of an alley, part of a potato in its jaws, and she gasped. A man in the shadows chuckled. Her heart raced; she raised her skirts and hurried on. A glance over her shoulder assured her no one followed.

A dim light glowed through the stable window. Mason's deep voice rumbled. She slipped inside and stopped.

A stranger with a broad hat and heavy leather gloves sat aloft, holding the reins of the loaded mule cart. A short rope tethered a horse to the rear of the cart. Neither Lin nor Eva in sight.

Mason stood to one side. "Don't forget to feed and water Bessie," he said. "You'll need to rest her every few hours. Take good care of her and she'll give you all she's got."

The stranger nodded and a woman's voice emerged from under the hat. "You're our guardian angel. Thank you for everything." Her chin tilted up and Eva's face appeared. Her gaze fell upon Jillian. "Come to wish us Godspeed?"

A rustle sounded from the back of the cart. A large tarp covered the load which must include a drugged Lin. How was this sheltered woman going to manage, with her soft hands and urban background? Would she even make it to the edge of the city? "I wish you luck."

Mason patted the mule's wide rump, then crossed to the stable doors. "Remember, slow and steady until you're out of town. You don't want to attract any attention."

Eva's shoulders stiffened. Her gloved hands gripped the reins as though at a lifeline. She slapped the reins against the mule's back and clicked her tongue. The cart rolled forward and onto the street. The horse followed behind.

"What do you think their chances are?" Jillian stood beside Mason, her arm tucked through his. The sweet smell of straw and oats blended with his musky odor.

"Fifty-fifty."

"You're generous."

"Lin called her a tiger. She'll need to get her claws out."

As the cart turned a corner and moved out of sight, Jillian closed her eyes, whispering a request for the universe to keep the couple safe.

Mason closed the stable doors. "Say one for us while you're at it."

"If they get caught, Lin will bring us back."

He nodded, his jaw tight. "He'll try."

"Also." She hesitated. "We may have another problem."

Mason paid close attention to her recap of Zeb's visit, frown lines deep at the edges of his mouth. Three years of rough life had aged him prematurely. "The Crockers are important people. If we're caught breaking into their home in the middle of the night, it will mean serious jail time for both of us."

She acknowledged this with a nod. "We can't wait until dawn. I'll be arrested then, for sure."

"We could run." His statement hung between them for a few breaths.

If it came to flight, where would they go? North to Canada, east toward Reno, her once and future home in Mendocino? Her heart ached for her tidy cottage that overlooked the rocky cliffs of the Pacific Ocean. Home didn't exist yet. Mason's home in Australia was even more remote.

"Is that what you want to do?"

He grasped her hands. "I don't want you to be in jail. We'd be taking a big risk, and neither of us knows how to break into a house. But...we have a chance at getting back to our old lives." He scratched his beard and a corner of his mouth quirked up. "I wouldn't mind a hot shower and a change of occupation. I'd like the feel of a camera in my hands again."

She swallowed and took a deep breath. Each option carried considerable risk. "Let's go break into the Crockers' house."

****

They waited an hour, long enough for Lin and Eva to leave the city limits. Mason wrote a note for Thomas to buy himself the fishing pole and a blueberry pie, and left twenty dollars for the boy, more than two months of earnings. Jillian added a few lines requesting he pick up her uniform at the Chinese laundry and return it to Mrs. March, as well as deliver payment to the dressmaker.

She added her remaining funds to Mason's. "Are you sure I can trust him to run these errands?"

"He's a good lad," he said with a nod.

A bright full moon rose above the treetops as they made their way to the Crocker mansion. Their path took them along quiet streets, away from where the busy saloons still conducted their lucrative first and second story businesses. Here, past darkened homes, only an occasional coyote howl in the distance broke the silence.

Jillian forced her pace to a stroll, as though they were no more than lovers on their way home and not on their way to commit a crime. Fear coursed through her. What if they couldn't get into the house tonight? What if the portal didn't work? What if it catapulted them further back in time, or to a future era where they didn't belong? There was more possibility of events going wrong than going right.

Beside her, Mason appeared equally tense. Jaw clenched, he kept a constant surveillance of their surroundings, with an occasional glance over his shoulder. An owl hooted and his head jerked up, before he gave a wry grin in recognition of his uneasiness.

A block from the mansion, the moon illuminated a small pond that had formed across the road from the rain and impeded their progress. They had no choice but to wade through the water. Jillian had hiked her skirts to her knees before Mason caught her up in his arms.

"What are you doing?"

Holding her close, he splashed through the water in long strides and set her down on the other side. "Isn't this the age of gallantry?"

She wrinkled her nose. "I don't think you have your country or century right."

"Don't I even get a thank you?"

She wrapped her arms around his neck, and kissed him hard, this good man who refused to allow adversity to degrade his character. He met her lips with alacrity and his grip around her waist tightened. The kiss renewed her determination and courage. His gaze reflected similar resolve. They *would* succeed. They *had* to.

He gripped her hand and tugged her forward. They rounded a corner and their pace quickened as they neared the mansion. The impressive estate gleamed under the moonlight. A swathe of well-clipped lawn fronted the home and a splendid magnolia tree, branches heavy with foliage, cast a shadow on one side. They stopped in its shelter and contemplated their next step.

"Windows on the first floor are locked tight at bedtime," Jillian explained. "The dining room is on the second level."

"Any ideas?"

"One possibility." Her gaze scanned the windows of the servants' house. She selected several pebbles at her feet, then emerged from the shadow to draw closer to the side of the structure. She hurled one of the small stones. It sailed wide and clattered against the wall. A second one also missed, looping off track, and it struck the family mansion where the bedrooms lay.

"This is sure to wake the household." Mason picked up a small rock, drew back his arm, and tossed it. The stone hit its mark. He grinned. "Youth cricket matches. I was always a top bowler."

The window slid open and Caleb's head appeared.

"Caleb, let us in," she hissed. "It's me, Jillian."

His mouth turned down as he peered at her and then Mason. "I can't do that. I'd be dismissed for sure. Crikey, you're in a heap of trouble."

Jillian leaned forward. "I have a gold nugget and a dollar that's all yours if you unlock the door. That's all you have to do. No one will accuse you of any wrongdoing."

He bit his lip and didn't respond. She pressed her advantage and flourished the marble-sized gold nugget, the biggest she'd received from her work at Lou's that night. She rolled it in her palm to catch the moonlight. His eyes widened. "One minute, Caleb. That's all."

"This is like that painting, ain't it? I can pick good or evil. Mr. Crocker says we live in the midst of both, and the choice is ours." He shook his head firmly. "No. I won't do it. Not for fifty gold nuggets."

The window slid shut and a lock snapped into place. She stepped back, dismayed by the boy's refusal as well as his belief she was immoral. They weren't there to steal or harm anyone, just…just to break in like common criminals. Her shoulders sagged. There had to be a way inside.

"What about one of the maids?" Mason asked.

"Sarah wouldn't, nor Mrs. March." She bit her lip. They'd have to force a lock.

Another window slid open bit by bit, this time from the family mansion. Small hands tugged at the pane. The younger Crocker daughter, Amy, peeked out. "You found each other. Are you back to haunt our house?"

Jillian clutched Mason's arm. Here was a way in. "Amy, we don't want to haunt anyone. We need to go inside the dining room, so we can…return to our own time."

The child tilted her head to one side. "Can't you walk through walls? In my books, ghosts can go anywhere they want."

"We aren't—" Jillian stopped. If she stood there talking, another window would soon open and their opportunity lost. "Please, unlock the door. I promise we don't mean any harm."

"If I do, will you answer three questions about what it's like to be ghosts?" The girl's face lit up. "It'd be like a genie from one of my books, granting me three wishes."

Jillian almost jumped up and down in frustration.

"Yes, but please hurry."

Amy's face disappeared from the window.

They rounded the corner toward the kitchen when she stopped. "Wait, she wouldn't come to the kitchen. As a family member, Amy would open the front door." They hurried back to the grand carved door and sure enough, within moments, a click indicated a bolt drawn back. The door gave a slight creak as it opened. Amy stood before them in a white nightgown, her feet bare, and her dark hair twisted into stubby braids.

The girl blocked the doorway with her body. "First question. What do you eat?"

Whatever it took to reach the portal, Jillian was happy to play along. "Whatever you can eat. But I'm craving a fresh caprese salad." She nodded to Mason, a gesture for him to humor the girl.

"I'd love a triple-stack hamburger on a seeded bun," he said.

Amy swung the door wider to allow them entry. "I've never heard of either one of those foods. I will write this down in my diary." She held a finger to her lips. "Be quiet or you'll frighten my mother. She also hears spirits but doesn't like them as much as I do."

They padded with soft steps across the entry to the dining room.

"Question two," Amy said, her voice barely above a whisper. "Why did you come here?"

Mason knelt down to her level. "We had a serious mission, a very important goal to accomplish. We needed to save two lives."

"Gee whiz," the girl breathed. "And did you? No, wait, that's not my last question."

"I'll answer it anyway. Yes, I believe we did."

Moonlight lit the room; Jillian crossed to the spot by the window, the same place she'd stood before. This had to work. Lin and Eva must be out of the city by now, so there should be no energy to block their return. "We need to go, right now, before we're discovered."

Mason joined her, grasping her hand. They interlocked fingers securely. She didn't want to think they might end up years or decades apart in the future.

"I have my third question ready," Amy said. "Where are you going?"

"Home," they answered together.

The ground trembled and a distant rumble sounded, like the roar of an oncoming train. The child's eyes grew wide. Jillian tightened her grip. Goosebumps rippled up and down her arms.

Thunder seemed to emanate from the walls. Once again, the ground rolled and heaved beneath her feet. A jolt wrenched her fingers loose from Mason's and the floor rose up to meet her as she fell. *Mason.* Shadows swallowed him up. The space around her darkest night, the moonlight quenched. *I'm falling. I'm falling.*

Then the roaring stopped and sunlight poured in.

Chapter Nineteen

A firm hand grasped Jillian's upper arm and tugged her to her feet. She met Mason's hazel gaze. Her heart leaped in relief.

"What the—?" A clatter drew their attention to a security guard in the doorway, the very same one who scolded her for taking photos. His face leached of color, at his feet a broken security radio. "Where—?" His mouth gaped open. He whirled and fled; his footsteps pounded and echoed through the museum.

Jillian took in her surroundings. The room was lined with glass cases, filled with vases and various items from the Victorian age. A faint aroma of lemon-scented furniture polish, the large chandelier with electric lights, the long dining table bare. Every detail exactly as the day she had left a week earlier.

"We did it," she breathed as tears stung her eyes. "We're back."

Mason's hand still gripped her upper arm. "I thought I'd lost you."

"Me, too." She pried his fingers loose from where they bruised her skin and kissed his knuckles. Her attention drew to an item at her feet. "This can't be possible. My phone. It's right here where I dropped it." She retrieved it with a frown, puzzled that no one had touched the phone or taken it to the security desk. "I think…I think I've only been gone a moment or two.

The guard must have seen me disappear and then reappear with you."

"No wonder he took off like that." Mason chuckled, a low sound that grew into a laugh.

She grinned. "Like he saw a ghost." She giggled and the corset squeezed her ribs. "And I'm in a completely different set of clothes."

They hung on to each other and laughed until tears ran. She leaned her head against his chest. *We're here, we did it.*

Jillian wiped her eyes as a sobering memory invaded her thoughts. Lin had never promised he wouldn't seize them again. "Let's get out of here."

As though he understood her fears, Mason nodded. "First, I want to see the painting. Once more."

They made their way to the grand gallery and surveyed Nahl's great work.

"I don't understand." Jillian's glance swept from one side to the other. "You aren't in the picture any longer. But you *were* there. Being back here doesn't change the fact that the artist met you and used you as a model."

Mason rubbed his beard. "I have the whiskers to prove we didn't imagine it."

"Do you think, somehow, time patched over our intrusion? So that we belong to solely one era, and we can't change history?"

"We *did* change the past. We freed Lin and reunited him with Eva."

This was a puzzle they might never solve.

"Did they make it, do you think?" she murmured.

Footsteps thudded up the stairs. A woman in Bermuda shorts and sandals gave them a smile as she passed. "I'm glad women don't have to wear all that garb anymore," she said. "They must have suffocated in the summertime."

Jillian agreed. "I can vouch for that fact."

The woman laughed and continued to the next floor, while Mason and Jillian hurried to the exit. Outside, they stopped in a small park next to the museum, where their period attire drew curious stares from passersby. The bench where they sat faced the entrance of the sleek modern structure. The servants' house no longer existed; in its place stood an elevated corridor. She kicked off her shoes and, with a quick glance around, undid her garters and worked her stockings down her thighs and off. Her toes sank into the cool grass.

"Oh, that feels amazing."

"I can't wait to get this off my face." Mason scratched his beard. "I'll need to shave or people will wonder how I grew this monster in two weeks."

"Your hair's gone a bit gray, too." Jillian examined his changed appearance: his muscled arms and thickened torso, deep tan, a few extra wrinkles at the edges of his eyes. "You'll have some explaining to do about your new physique."

His lips twitched in amusement. "A fitness boot camp?"

A breeze carried scents of wildflowers and automobile exhaust, a modern blend so pervasive that it never before rose to her consciousness. She closed her eyes and took a deep breath. Gratitude flooded through her. So much could have gone wrong over the past week. She might never have found Mason, Lin might have died or been shipped back to China, the opportunity to reenter the Crocker mansion blocked. And then, that awful moment when Mason's hand slipped from her grasp and she believed him lost to her again.

"I never fully explained why I wanted to surprise you in Sacramento."

Jillian opened her eyes at Mason's words and squeezed his hand. She leaned her head against his broad shoulder, so much more substantial after his work as a miner and blacksmith. "It became more of a surprise than ever."

He shifted and she lifted her head. His gaze bored into her. "I had it all planned out. The train ride through the Sierra Nevada range, a stay in Reno, maybe a stopover in Tahoe on the way back."

"Oh, I can't wait for a soft mattress and a glass of wine." She tugged at her middle. "My own clothes. I'm desperate to get this corset off. I'd like to take a deep breath."

Around them people—*modern* people—wandered about. A man wore a baseball cap, a woman cycled toward the river in a bathing suit, teens held hands. Music blasted from a passing car. A nearby freeway produced a steady roar. All of it proof they were back where they belonged.

"Jillian." Mason's tone drew her attention. His throat worked and his fingers picked at stitches in his pants' waistband. "After the past week—or three years—or whatever it's been—now, more than ever, I know there's no other woman in the world for me. When I offered to marry Eva, you don't know how I suffered."

Her mouth dried up. "I don't blame you. Okay,

maybe for one minute, but then I realized it had been three years for you. I would have stayed; even shared you with that—"

She stopped as his hand rose between them. Between his thumb and forefinger was a solitaire diamond ring; the facets caught the sunlight and sparkled. "I almost lost this several times over the past three years, but something in me kept faith that somehow I'd see you again."

Tears blurred her vision. "You...kept this...all this time? When you were hungry and homeless?" He'd carried a ring, a promise to keep faith to her, for three years of hardships and hopelessness.

"I intended to propose on the train, but I was...delayed. Then I vowed to help Eva and couldn't break that promise. And I believed I'd never see you again. Now, more than before, you should know my heart is yours, whatever century we're in. Jillian Winchester, wherever you go, I'm willing to follow. Tell me, will you marry me?"

She swallowed the lump in her throat. "I would have stayed and been your mistress if things ended up differently. I can't imagine life without you." She stretched out her left hand. "My heart is bound to yours. Of course, I'll marry you."

He slipped on the ring and then his lips burned against hers, bruising them with intensity. His arms crushed her close and her breath quickened, constrained by the corset.

"I'm going to faint," she said, half laughing and half gasping.

An older couple strolled by, their path angled toward the museum entrance. The woman's eyes crinkled. "They hired people in period costume today. What fun!"

Jillian grabbed Mason's hand. "Let's go home."

****

She couldn't stop reveling in modern conveniences. Flush toilets, a *dishwasher*, online shopping; dozens of times a day, the disparity between past and present surfaced. And this kept alive Lin's words: *I can't promise our paths won't cross again.*

Mason bounced back to his previous life without trouble. Scarcely fifteen days after their return, he traveled on assignment to Africa for an outdoor magazine. He couldn't wait to get a camera back in his hands and return to his career. For her, flashbacks caught her unawares. Her time in the past was far shorter than Mason's but she struggled with memories and nightmares. Would the next spirit she met take her captive?

Jillian took her morning tea out to the back deck, which overlooked the pounding surf of the Pacific Ocean. She sipped the hot liquid, the aroma of a eucalyptus-mango blend that drifted up from the mug. The diamond on her finger glinted and shone, a promise and reminder of Mason's faithfulness. They hadn't set a date. As far as she was concerned, they didn't need one. Their paths merged already—a ceremony or marriage certificate superfluous.

She'd taken a hiatus from her Spirited Quest blog, fearful that somehow writing about her experiences would conjure Lin and Eva back into their lives. She closed her mind to spirits and considered a new career, though nothing called to her. Lin's hint that he might summon them back kept her on edge. Would it be tomorrow, or a year from now? There had been no mention of Lin or Eva in internet searches, and no way to know if they had even survived their flight. Danger might have arrived too swiftly for Lin to reach out to her and Mason for help. Or they lived long and uneventful lives, secreted somewhere far from prejudice and harm.

Seagulls wheeled on air currents above the waves. Their calls and easy circling patterns soothed her disquiet. Damp salt air licked at her hair and face.

"Give it time," Mason told her before he left. "You'll know when you're ready to resume your blog."

Not yet. Maybe never.

"Hello?"

A young woman peered around the side of her house, a sleek bicycle at her side. Attired in black shorts and a yellow racing jersey, she had long ebony hair and light green eyes.

The woman advanced a couple of steps and halted. "I'm sorry if I startled you. No one answered the door and I thought…I thought if I had a house that faced the ocean, I might be outside." She leaned the bicycle against the house and approached the bottom of the deck's stairs.

Jillian's heart thumped back to a normal rhythm. Tourists besieged the small seaside town in the summer and often sought directions or information from locals—on a few occasions, even picnicked on her property. "I never get tired of the view," she agreed. "Can I help you? Are you lost?"

The woman gave a small laugh as though embarrassed. In one hand she held an envelope, yellowed with age. "I'm sure this is a mistake, but could you be Jillian Winchester?"

"You're at the right spot." Something about the woman set Jillian's heart back to racing. Fine hairs on her arms stood up.

The woman's eyes widened. "Seriously? There really *is* a Jillian Winchester? We all assumed this was a prank." The paper in her hand crinkled. "I-I have a letter for you. This is crazy." She mounted the steps and handed over the envelope.

Jillian's name was written in elaborate script on the front of the sealed envelope. "Who is this from?"

"Okay, this is the truth so don't think I'm a lunatic." She wrinkled her nose on which a tiny stud decorated the side of one nostril. "This letter has been passed down in my family for eighty years, with instructions to deliver it to a Jillian Winchester on this date. My great-great grandmother wrote it, on her deathbed, I believe."

The woman gave another embarrassed laugh. "It's been sort of a family joke. Except a clause in her will makes the next generation swear to pass it along. I inherited it a couple of months ago and signed up for a race in the area. So, well, here I am. But there's no way you ever knew her." She handed over a piece of paper and pen. "I need you to sign this affidavit to prove I delivered the letter."

Jillian scrawled her signature on the bottom of the document and handed it back. The woman clutched the paper to her chest.

The envelope weighed heavily in her hands. Stranger occurrences had happened, and she'd met any number of ghosts who might have addressed a letter to the far future. But the instruction to deliver the letter *now* gave her the strongest hint about who wrote it. Eighty years ago; yes, she could still have been alive. "Your great-great grandmother wouldn't have been Eva McAlister, would she?"

The woman's eyes widened, and she glanced around. "Her name was Eva Lee. But I believe her maiden name was McAlister. How did you know?"

"It's a long story. There's a connection, from way back. It's complicated." Jillian studied the woman in front of her, who appeared uncomfortable with the situation and eager to leave. Those light green eyes reminiscent of Eva's cool gaze. "Please, would you like to come in?"

"I researched you. You write about ghosts. Like I said, I thought this was a prank. But you're real." She held up both hands and backed away. "Everyone said my great-great grandfather was the one who meddled with the supernatural. I don't want to get involved with whatever this is."

To be honest, neither did she. A sense of foreboding swept through her. There couldn't be a trace of goodness in any letter Eva penned.

The young woman hoisted a backpack that lay next to the bicycle onto her shoulders. "I did what my aunt asked in her will. That's all I need to do in order to inherit my share of the family fortune." She flicked her hair over her shoulder and retrieved her bike. "*Ciao.*"

"Thank you," Jillian called to the woman's departing back. Her outright rejection of the supernatural recalled to mind Eva's reaction to the concept of time travel. Both women so very sure of themselves.

A hummingbird, its throat a brilliant emerald and

sapphire, buzzed past like a giant bumblebee and hovered before a cluster of hanging fuchsias. It twisted and stared at Jillian before it zipped away. She clutched the envelope. The thick paper crinkled in her hands. The seal unbroken. Its contents and the strange instructions that accompanied it must have evoked keen curiosity over the decades.

Was this a summons to return to the 1800s? If she broke the seal, would the action catapult her back in time once more? Might Mason already be there, in danger? She stripped open the seal and lifted the flap. She held her breath and waited. Nothing. Waves crashed against the rocky shore below, and seagulls screeched in the distance. Still here.

She took a deep breath and withdrew five pages from the envelope.

Chapter Twenty

Eva must have written the letter over a course of days or weeks, the handwriting varied as though the writer stopped and started anew at various times. At places the words bunched in a tight scrawl almost illegible and at others in a wide flowing script.

Jillian flipped to the first page and began:

Nov. 29, 1942

Dear Jillian,

Seventy years have come and gone since our little adventure in Sacramento. Next month I will be ninety and there's considerable doubt I'll achieve that milestone. If I don't set this down now, I never will.

Are you surprised to hear from me? After all, I didn't believe your fairy tale story in my younger days. Over time, I've had plenty of opportunity to experience the strangeness of life as well as many hours of contemplation. Lin shared his own gift and his role in conveying you and Mason to our time. I believe all you told me, and a great deal more.

Lin has been gone for twenty-three years and I miss him terribly. He convinced me in the end that we will see each other again, and I believe that is true. If I can believe that, then why not stories about time travel and ghosts?

If you are reading this, you have met one of my relatives. I hope that person is a good representative of my family, handsome or beautiful, well-behaved and cultured. I am a very rich woman and in a position to provide a sizable reward to future heirs for making sure this epistle reaches your hands.

I've gone to this effort for two reasons. The first is to tell you this: Lin never recalled you to the past.

A sob escaped Jillian. The hard knot of tension that had resided in her stomach for two weeks loosened. She swiped away tears that blurred her vision. A breeze ruffled the pages; she gripped them and continued to read, this time more avidly.

After Lin passed away, it weighed more and more on my mind, that you would spend your life in dread of another abduction. I owe you this favor, and more, as you will come to discover as you read on.

Lin and I had fourteen children, eleven of whom survived into adulthood. All eleven married and had children, and so on. If I survive the winter, I may witness the birth of my first great great grandchild. I've lost count of the number of family members and can't remember most of their names. I do remember you and Mason, though, just as if it all happened yesterday.

Your predictions came true—telephones, motorcars, electricity, airplanes. Year after year, unbelievable miracles. Each fell into place like a string of pearls.

The ink changed from blue to black and the handwriting worsened into a scrawl. She crossed the deck to a patio chair and sank upon the faded red-checked cushion.

After you and Mason departed, Lin and I traveled for four months without pause for more than a night or two. We had no destination other than to get as far away as possible from Sacramento. Those months were difficult beyond measure.

Jillian recalled how unprepared Eva was for a life of rough living. There must have been a steely resolve that surfaced, and a determination to be with Lin. The letter detailed their dash into the vast wilds of the Sierra Nevada range, bug bites and near starvation, as well as a growing aptitude for the survivalist life. Lin suffered through opium withdrawal for weeks before the need eased.

"I had to do nearly everything at first. We were fortunate because it was the summer season. Fish swam in the streams, wild berries abundant, and star-filled nights guided us. By the time I grew too heavy to do much, Lin prevailed over his addiction. Our son was born a month after we crossed into Canada. We never were able to legally marry but we chose a common last name, Lee, that made sense for us both. We lived in areas where people minded their own business. Once Lin began making a fortune in oil, the money and the power it produced sheltered us from most forms of discrimination.

Such a quandary time travel is. I pen this missive to a person I met years ago but who isn't yet born. The stuff of movies (another modern invention I enjoy very much).

The handwriting changed again, the ink darker on the page as though the writer spent more time on each word.

I hope you and Mason find the same love Lin and I enjoyed for so many years. We spoke of both of you often, though just between the two of us as no one else would believe us. I came to realize what a great wrong

Lin did. He snatched you from your time and disrupted your lives. I didn't understand the fear and desperation you must have felt. This weighed more on my heart as I grew older and at times created quarrels between us. Lin insisted he had no other choice. I contended we may have unknowingly changed the future for the worse by our actions. One day, he ended our arguments by relating the events aboard a ship when he sailed from China to San Francisco as a teenager.

I come to the second reason I write this letter. Lin kept a secret from all of us. While on the ship, he fell ill and almost died. At the height of his fever, when he was given up for dead, he journeyed through time. This is when he foresaw the four of us together and the repercussions of our encounter on future events. He knew he would find me, and you and Mason fated to save us. Of course, the path might have been smoother had he foreseen the trap his brothers set for him. But his visions don't show him everything, only the path he may choose to take. During his illness, he traveled further into the future and witnessed even more.

Oh, the future! Great changes are still in store for mankind. My heart both aches and soars with the knowledge Lin shared. He visited a dozen generations in front of us. And there he found one of our descendants at the juncture of a very dark time in history. There is so much you didn't share with me—the world wars, Depression, the terrible Spanish flu that took one of our grandchildren. Likewise, I won't tell you of the grim days ahead. Frankly, you'll be gone by then anyway. All I will relate is someone terrible— someone monstrous—will not rise to power, because of one of our descendants.

Jillian set down the letter. If this were true, why did Lin keep such critical information a secret? Was it because their actions set the stage for a far-future coup or murder, and he feared their reluctance to participate? They would have none but Lin's perspective on future events to trust. Perhaps they would have asked too many questions, delayed the rescue, and ruined everything.

The remainder of the letter detailed successes of Eva and Lin's children and grandchildren, marriages and a mid-life reconciliation with Lin's brothers. Jillian tucked the letter away. She must call Mason later to tell him the news, and he could read it upon his return. For the first time in weeks, her fingers itched to write down her experiences. The sensation sent a thrill through her and drove her inside to open her computer.

Readers believed when she wrote about spirits, but time travel was different. How would they react to this adventure? There was one way to find out. She began to type.

From the Spirited Quest blog:

Dear readers,

I've been on a long journey that rattled my beliefs and struck me to the core. It nearly took me away from you forever, into a place where I was the spirit. Let me tell you all about it…

A word about the author...

Julie Howard is the author of the Wild Crime and Spirited Quest series. She is a former journalist and editor who has covered topics ranging from crime to cowboy poetry.

She is a member of the Idaho Writers Guild and founder of the Boise chapter of Shut Up & Write.

Learn more at:

juliemhoward.com